Nightpool

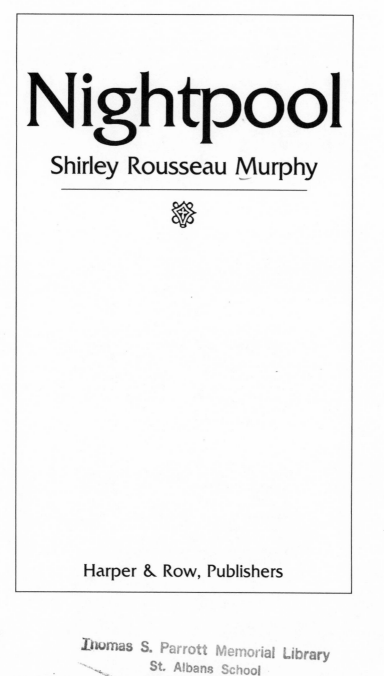

Nightpool

Shirley Rousseau Murphy

Harper & Row, Publishers

Library of Congress Cataloging in Publication Data
Murphy, Shirley Rousseau.
    Nightpool.

    Summary: Injured in battle with the Dark
Raiders, sixteen-year-old Tebriel is healed by a
colony of talking otters and sets out to fight the
Dark and its forces of evil in the world of Tirror.
    [1. Fantasy]   I. Title
PZ7.M956Ni 1985   [Fic]   85-42626
ISBN 0-06-024360-0
ISBN 0-06-024361-9 (lib. bdg.)

For Darby and Welch Suggs

1

It was early dawn when a swimmer appeared far out in the dark, rolling sea. His face was just visible, a pale smear, and his hair blended with the black waves. He dove suddenly and disappeared, then was hidden by scarves of blowing fog stained pale in the moonlight. Moonlight brightened the crashing spray, too, where waves shattered against the tall, rocky island.

The swimmer popped up again, close to the island's cliff. He breasted the waves and foam with strong strokes and leaped to grab at the sheer stone wall. A foothold here, a handhold, until his wet naked body was free of the sea, clinging like a barnacle to the cliff. A thin boy, perhaps sixteen. He climbed fast, more from habit than from need, knowing just where the best holds were. Above him, the cliff was honeycombed

1

with caves, this whole side of the island a warren of dwellings, but no creature stirred above him. Not one dark, furred face looked out at him, and no otter hunted behind him in the sea; they all slept, after last night's ceremonies.

He climbed to his own cave and stood in the entrance dripping, his head ducked to clear the rough arch of the doorway. Then he turned back to look out at the sea once more. Behind him, his cave echoed the sea's pounding song.

He was bony and strong, with long, lean muscles laid close beneath the flesh, a thin face with high cheekbones, and his dark hair streaked and bleached by sun and sea. The skin across his loins, where the breechcloth had grown small for him, was pale, and the white scars on his back would never tan. His eyes were as dark as the stone of the island. There was a white, jagged scar across his chin, where a wave had heaved him against the cliff when he was twelve. He stood trying to master the flood of emotions that still gripped him, though he had thought to swim away from them out in the cold, dark sea. Homesickness was on him even before he departed, and he wanted to go quickly now while dawn lay on the sea and the otters slept, wanted no more good-byes, because already his stomach felt hollow and knotted. A part of himself would never go away, would stay on Nightpool forever, a ghost of himself still swimming the sea with Charkky

2

and Mikk, diving deep into undersea gardens, playing keep-away in the waves.

He longed to be with Mitta suddenly, gentle, mothering Mitta, who had cared for him all the long months he had lain sick and hurt and not knowing who he was, cared for him as tenderly as she cared for her own cubs. Maybe he could just slip up over the rim of the island and into her cave, and lay his face against her warm fur as she slept. But no, the good-byes would begin all over, and they had said good-bye. Maybe the worst part of leaving was the good-byes, even in the warmth and closeness they had all felt last night at the ceremony.

He thought of the monster he meant to seek, and fear touched him. But he felt power, too, and a stubbornness that would not let him imagine losing against the dark sea creature. And once he defeated it, his real journey would begin, for he went to seek not one, but two creatures, as unlike one another as hatred is unlike love.

His head filled again with last night's scene in the great cave. Before the ceremonies began, while he and Thakkur were alone there, the white otter had stood tall before the sacred clamshell pronouncing in a soft voice the visions that gave shape to Teb's searching. The gleaming, pale walls of the great cave had been lighted by fire for the first time the otters could remember, five small torches of flaming seaweed that

Charkky and Mikk had devised in Teb's honor. Teb thought of Thakkur's blessings and his strange, luminous predictions, the old otter's white sleek body stretched tall, his attention rooted to the shell.

"You will ride the winds of Tirror, Tebriel. And you will touch humankind and change it. You will see more than any creature or human sees, save those of your own special kind.

"I see mountains far to the north, and you will go there among wonderful creatures and speak to them and know them."

As Teb stared out now at the dawn sky, he was filled with the dream. But with the knowledge, too, that no prediction is cast in stone, that any fate could change by the flick of a knife, or the turn of a mount down an unknown road.

And not all Thakkur's predictions had been of wonder. "I see a street in Sharden's city narrow and mean. There is danger there and it reeks of pain. Take care, Tebriel, when you journey into Sharden.

"And," the white otter said softly, "I see your sister Camery, tall and golden as wheat, and I see a small owl on her shoulder." This was a happier prediction, and Teb vowed again that besides fulfilling his own search, he could find Camery, too, and those who traveled with her.

When Thakkur finished his predictions, Teb took his paw and walked with him down from the dais to a stone bench, where they sat together until, a little

4

later, the crowds of otters began to troop in. "Camery is alive," Teb said softly to Thakkur, and studied the white otter's whiskered face.

The white otter nodded briefly. And then, partly from old age and partly from the strain of the predictions, he lapsed into a sudden light, dozing sleep. Soon Teb was surrounded by otters and drawn away into a happy ceremony of gift giving.

Each otter had brought a gift, a shell carefully cleaned and polished, or a pawful of pearls, or a gold coin from the sunken city of Mernmeth, that had lain drowned for so many lifetimes with its treasures scattered across the ocean floor.

Now, as he stood looking out at the sea, the ceremony of gift giving began to form a song in his mind. His verses came quickly, pummeling into his head, and each made a picture of the giver, holding forth a treasure. The song would remain in his memory without effort, creating sharp, clear scenes that he could bring forth whenever he wished. Just so did hundreds of songs remain, captured somehow by that strange, effortless talent that set him apart from other humans. Always he carried in his mind this hoard of color and scenes and voices from the past.

He would carry with him on his journey, as well, a stolen leather pack, a stolen knife and sword, and the oaken bow that Charkky and Mikk had helped him make. He would carry the gold coins and pearls for trading, but the rest of the gifts would be left in his cave as intended, as good-luck omens to bring him back again, each carefully placed on the stone shelves carved into his cave walls, where Camery's diary lay wrapped in waterproof sharkskin. He had read it until he had worn out the pages.

He would need to steal a new flint for fire making, for he had given his to Charkky and Mikk. And he would have to steal some clothes, for he had only his breechcloth and his old leather tunic with the seams let out. He had no boots, and the cliffs and rocky, stubbled pastures would be harsh going. He would steal, not trade, until he was well away from the lands where he might be known.

He lay down on his sleeping shelf to measure his length and pressed his feet and head against the stone, then drew himself up small, the length he had been when he first came to live in this cave. He sat up and touched the woven gull-feather blanket at the foot of the shelf. The blanket had been Mitta's first large weaving; many otters had gathered its feathers, and she had labored a long time over it. The otters had done so many things for him that they had never done before; many that were against their customs. It didn't seem right to have brought such change to the otter folk, then to leave as if he cared nothing for them, or for the way they had sheltered him and taught him.

He had brought change to Nightpool unwanted by many: the planting of crops, the way small things were done, the tools and weapons of humans. He had brought fire, brought the cooking of food, so that even last night the ceremonial feast had been of both the traditional raw seafood laid out on seaweed—clams and oysters and mussels and raw fish—and then a pot set over the fire to steam the shellfish, too.

The stealing had been the biggest change, and many otters had been angry about that first theft, though Charkky and Mikk had thought it a rare adventure. And even Thakkur, later on, had been very keen about stealing weapons, covering his white fur with mud so he could not be seen in the night.

It pleased Teb to know that no one else, no human, would take his place in the otter nation; no other human would sleep in his cave or dive deep into the sea among a crowd of laughing otters. Thakkur's faith that he would return pleased him. "You will know your cave is here, Tebriel, waiting for you, filled with your possessions." Yet Teb knew well enough he might never return, in a future as malleable as the changing directions of the sea.

But once he swam the channel, once he stood on the shore, then climbed the cliff to Auric's fields, his commitment would be made. Once he defeated the sea hydrus—if, indeed, he could defeat it—he would not return soon to the black rock island, to Nightpool's sea winds and the green, luminous world of undersea, to the weightless freedom of the sea. If he could defeat the hydrus, he knew he would then be drawn out across the wild, warring lands of Tirror. Deep within his being the call grew even stronger, and his need to give of himself to Tirror grew bold.

He stood listening to the voice of his cave echo the roaring beat of the sea. There would be no cave song on dry land, only the voices of land animals. And the voices of men, very likely challenging him.

When he turned from the sea back into his cave, the white otter was coming silently along the narrow ledge, erect on his hind legs, his whiteness startling against the black stone, his forepaws folded together and very still, not fussing as other otters' paws fussed. Thakkur paused, quietly watching him, and Teb knelt at once, in a passion of reverence quite unlike himself. But Thakkur frowned and reached out a paw to touch Teb's shoulder; their eyes were on a level now, Thakkur's dark eyes half laughing, half annoyed. "Get up, Teb. Do not kneel before me." Then his look went bright and loving.

Teb stood up and turned away into the cave, embarrassed, and busied himself readying his pack, then pulling on his tunic.

"You have grown so tall, Tebriel. It was not long ago that I was taller than you." The look between them was easy, a look of love and of sadness. "I have come to say a last farewell. Not good-bye, for I know you will return to Nightpool."

"No prophesy is absolute."

"This vision is strong. You will return, I have no doubt of it." The white otter's dark eyes were as deep and fathomless as the sea itself. "But now the time has come, now you must go, and from this moment you belong not only to Nightpool, but to all of Tirror. Your fate lies upon Tirror now. Both Tirror's fate, and our own fate, travels with you."

They embraced, the white otter's fur infinitely soft against Teb's face, and smelling of sea and of sun.

"Go in joy, Tebriel. Go with the blessing of The Maker. Go in the care of the Graven Light."

Teb took up his pack at last and lashed it to his waist. He gave Thakkur a long, steady look, then stepped to the edge of the cliff and dove far out and deep, cutting the water cleanly and striking out at once against the incoming swells. As quickly as that he left Nightpool, and his tears mixed with the salty sea.

At a safe distance from the cliffs he turned north, and glancing up between strokes, he caught a glimpse of Thakkur's white form on the black island; then the vision vanished in a shattering of green water as he made his way with strong, pulling strokes crosswise to the force of the sea, up toward the north end of the island.

He could have walked across Nightpool and swum the channel from the mainland side, but not this morning, not this last time. As he passed the lower caves at the far end of the island, he could hear water slapping into the cave doors. At the far end, beside Shark Rock, he turned again, toward land this time, and set out in an easier rhythm with the tide, to cross the deep green channel. And it was here that suddenly two brown heads popped up beside him, and two grinning faces. Mikk and Charkky rolled and dove beside him, escorting him in toward the shore.

They leaped and splashed and pushed at him, rocked him on their own waves and dove between his feet and under him, and Charkky tickled his toes. Teb was not wearing the precious sharkskin flippers; he had left them safe in his cave. Charkky came up on his other side, dove again, was gone a long time, and came up ahead of Teb and Mikk with a sea urchin in each dark paw, busily stripping off the spines with his teeth. He tossed one to Mikk and one to Teb, and they were into a fast, complicated game of catch. Then when the game grew old, the two otters rolled onto their backs, cracked the urchins open with small stones they carried on cords around their necks, and ate them live and raw. Teb tried to outdistance them, but without the flippers he hadn't a chance, even when they only floated idly kicking and eating.

They left him before the sea shallowed onto rising shore, embracing him in quick, strong, fishy-smelling hugs and dragging their rough whiskers hard across his cheek, their eyes great dark-brown pools of longing and of missing him, and of love, and of silly otter humor all at once.

"Fly high, brother," Mikk said hoarsely. "Know clouds, brother, as you know the sea." They studied one another with love and concern.

Charkky just touched his cheek, softly, with a wet, gentle paw. Then they were gone, diving down along the bottom, dropping deeper, Teb knew, as the shore dropped, swimming deep toward home.

Teb stood up in the shallow water and walked up the shore. The beach was narrow, steep, and rocky. Above him rose the tall cliff, and against the sky lay the lip of the rich high pastures of Auric, a green thatch hanging over the edge. His father's pastures, he thought with sudden emotion. His father's land—his own land these four years since his father was murdered, though he had no way to claim it. I am King of Auric, he thought bitterly. And I stand on Auric's shore naked and alone, and the dark warriors would try to kill me if they knew. If Sivich and his soldiers knew I was here, they would ride down from the castle to kill me. He smiled and felt his sword, and almost wished they would try.

Then he shook himself, stood a moment to dry in the wind, and began to climb the cliff.

It was steep, but the outcropping stones and tough hanks of dry grass helped him. As he pulled himself over the edge, something snorted, and a band of horses shied and wheeled nearly on top of him, and pounded away across the hills.

Why hadn't he been more careful? Why hadn't he looked before he let himself be seen? He might have had himself a mount now if he'd used his head. And what if it had been soldiers? It was not a good begin-

11

ning. As he swung up over the lip of the cliff, he re-
solved to take more care.

He stood looking out across the rolling green hills
and at the little villages far distant along the west
turning of the coast. Inland to the west, between two
familiar hills and a grove of almond trees, stood the
towers of home, stood the Palace of Auric. His memories crowded back, sweeping him away into scenes
that were, each, a stabbing pain. It all flooded back,
the beatings and the leg chains from which he still
wore scars, the cruelty of Sivich and his guards. He
stood brooding and angry, filled with the pain of his
father's murder, with the helpless fury holding him
now as if no time had passed, as if he and Camery
were still prisoners in their dead father's palace. He
remembered it all in every detail, the pain, the stink
of the unkempt palace, remembered as if he were twelve
again, chained in the cold stone cellar. Remembered . . .

2

He had been barely twelve years old, a small, thin boy sleeping on the stone floor of a prison cell so deep in the cellars of the palace you could not tell night from day. It was near midnight when the guard's boot nudged his ribs. His eyes flew open; then he squeezed them closed in the bright lantern light and curled tighter beneath the thin blanket he had doubled and tucked around himself. When the boot nudged harder, insistently, he scowled up into the light again and into Blaggen's sleep-puffy face, lit from beneath by the swinging flame. Blaggen smelled of liquor, as usual, and of leather wet from his own urine, for he had dirty ways. The two guard jackals pushed closer to Teb, mixing their own rank smell, like spoiled meat, with Blaggen's, their little mean eyes red in the light and their wings dragging the floor with a dusty dry sound. They were heavier than Teb, and pushy. They slept in his cell and followed him in all his serving duties, their slavering grins eager for him to try escape.

Blaggen kicked him again, so hard it took his breath. Teb squirmed out of the tangle of blanket, confused and clumsy, but could not tear himself fully from sleep.

"Get up, son of pigs. Sivich wants you in the hall. There are soldiers to serve, thirsty from a long ride." He emphasized *thirsty* with another nudge. Teb wanted to hit him, but knew better. The welts on his back still pained him from his last outburst of fury. Blaggen belched into his yellow beard and, tired of watching the boy squirm under his boot, jerked him up by the collar, jerked the cell door open with an echoing clang, and shoved Teb before him down the narrow black passage. Up three flights, Teb stumbling in darkness on the stone steps, the jackals crowding close.

In the hall the torches were all ablaze, and a great fire burned on the hearth. The room was filled with warriors, shouting and arguing and laughing. Sivich paced before the fire, his broad, black-bearded head jutting like a mean-tempered bull's. Weapons were piled beside the outer door that led down to the court-yard: heavy swords; long, curved bows and leather quivers filled with arrows; and the oak-shafted spears.

Teb crossed to the scullery at once. Old Desma was there, yawning and pushing back her gray hair, doubt-less dragged from sleep in the servants' quarters just as he had been dragged from sleep in his cell. The deep window behind her was black with night, but a wash of light shone from the courtyard below, and he heard hooves clattering on stone and bridles jingling as the warriors' horses were tended, then the echo of a man swearing; then a horse screamed. Desma glanced toward Blaggen and saw he had turned away. She put her arm around Teb and drew him to her comfortingly. Her old eyes were puffy from sleep. "I don't like this midnight riding, I don't like their talk. . . ." Then she broke off and pushed him away, because Blaggen had turned to look. She shoved a tray into Teb's hands and began to pile on silver mugs, two and three to a stack, and a heavy clay jug of mithnon. As she turned Teb toward the door, she whispered, "Get away from the palace. Get away tonight if you can."

"But how? How can I? Will you . . . ?"

She touched his face gently, her look was sad and closed. "I don't know how. There's no way I can help; they watch me too closely. He's looking—pretend I'm scolding you."

Teb left the pantry scowling and stumbling as if the old lady had been chiding him, and moved out among the elbowing men to serve up the dark, strong liquor.

He shuffled about holding the tray up to whoever shouted for it, and no one paid him much more attention, except to snatch up mugs and pour liquor, and berate him when the jug was empty. It shamed him to serve his father's murderers. Before they had killed his father, these men had treated him with oily, smiling deference. He wished it were poison he carried instead of mithnon, and he promised himself for the hundredth time that when he was grown, these men would die by his hand. Each of them would die, and Sivich would die slowly, with great pain.

When at last the men settled around Sivich before the fire, the edge of their thirst dulled and their mugs refilled, Blaggen motioned Teb away to his corner. Teb's arms ached from the heavy trays. He crouched against the stone wall on a bit of torn rug, the hump-shouldered jackals crowding close, and stared up through the small, barred window. A few stars shone in the black sky, and faint moonlight touched the tower, but he could see no movement within, and he imagined his sister asleep, curled up with her stuffed cloth owl. Once there had been a real owl, small and fat and filled with owlish humor. But Sivich had had the jackals kill it.

Now the two jackals began to bicker between themselves with low, menacing growls, pacing and hunching around Teb, their lips drawn back over long yellow teeth, the mottled, greasy hair along their spines rising in anger. They always pressed against Teb when they quarreled, and sometimes, snapping at one another, they bit him as well. He pulled away from them and huddled against the cold stone wall. The warriors were all talking at once, trying to tell Sivich something, shouting and swearing. What was the wonder they kept boasting about? *What* had flown over them? Teb had heard only snatches of talk as he served the liquor, a few words, questions broken by shouts for more drink. Now at last, one man at a time began to speak out under Sivich's questioning, Sivich's own voice sharp with excitement as the dark leader moved back and forth before the flicking tongues of flame.

"*Where* on the coast? *Exactly* where?" Sivich growled. "Are you sure it wasn't a hydrus? What . . . ?"

"East of the crossing. It was almost daylight. We saw . . ."

"It flew, I tell you. Can't no hydrus fly through the air. And there ain't no common dragon *that* big. Nor that color. Never."

Teb shivered, straining to hear.

"Not a common dragon. Big. Bright. It—" Pischen's voice broke as if the thin, wiry man were overcome with emotion. "Pearl colored, its scales all pearl and silver, and it reflected the firelight when it came down at us, all red and spitting flame, too. . . ."

"Horns as long as a man's arm," someone shouted.

Teb's heart raced. They were describing a singing dragon. No other creature would be that color, and so big. But were there any singing dragons left in Tirror? He could imagine it there in the sky, yes, huge, a dragon as luminous and iridescent as the sea opal, its great delicate head finely carved, its luminous horns flashing in the firelight. Was it really a singing dragon they saw? Or only a common dragon, wet from the

17

sea, reflecting the light of their campfire?

Even before the five wars began, no one knew whether a singing dragon still lived anywhere in Tirror. Yet Teb had dreamed that one might lurk, hidden and secret, in the tallest, wildest mountains far to the north. He and Camery had stopped talking about dragons, though, after their mother died. Their father didn't like such talk, particularly in front of others, his soldiers or the palace staff. He would hush them with an abrupt turn of the conversation, or send them on an errand.

Well, Teb was used to his father's anger, after his mother died. First she had gone away, and his father had *let* her go, had not gone after her, which Teb could never understand. Then his mother had drowned all alone, in the tide of the Bay of Fendreth, when her boat capsized. Though what she was doing there in a boat Teb had never known. And how she could have drowned, when she was such a strong swimmer, was always a puzzle to him. Except, that afternoon had been one of terrible storm and gale winds.

It was a sheep farmer who saw her struggling and, in his little skiff, tried to reach her. He searched the sea for her body, finding only her cloak and one boot. He brought the cloak and boot to the gate just at dusk, his old eyes filled with tears.

If Teb's father wept, he did not let Teb and Camery see his tears. He was stern and silent with the children after her death, locking all his pain inside. It would have been easier if they all could have shared their grief.

The king laid cloak and boot in a small gold cask set with coral, which had held his wife's favorite possessions. He buried the cask at the foot of the flame tree in her walled, private garden, and put a marker there, for her grave.

After that his father was often absent from the palace, busy at council with his lieutenants, planning war against the dark northern raiders that preyed upon Tirror's small nations and were drawing ever closer to Auric. It seemed strange to see him at council without the queen by his side, for they had always shared such duties. As he planned his defenses, pacing among his men, he seemed so filled with fury—almost as if he thought the dark raiders themselves were responsible for the queen's death.

Then his lieutenant, Sivich, gone suddenly and inexplicably over to the dark side, had, with a band of armed traitors, attacked the king and killed him. Sivich had always seemed so loyal. He must have lived a lie all those years, cleverly hiding his true intentions. Teb was there when it happened. He fought the traitors beside his father until he was knocked unconscious. He had been put into a cell and made a slave, and Camery locked in the tower. From the tower, and from the door of the palace, they saw their father buried in the courtyard in an unmarked grave.

At first Camery's pet owl had flown secretly at night

between the two children, whispering their messages through the tower window and through the barred window in the hall, until Sivich overheard and sent the jackals to kill the owl.

He expected Camery had cried a long time, for Otus had been a dear friend. Once the messages stopped, Teb yearned more and more to be with Camery, longed for her to hold him, for she was the closest thing to a mother he had left. Now he yearned to tell her about the dragon, for news of such a creature, if in truth it was a singing dragon, was surely a symbol of hope.

"Its shadow made the beach go dark," crippled Hibben was saying. "It screamed over the horses and made them bolt."

Sivich had risen and begun to pace, his shadow riding the worn tapestries back and forth. "How long was it in sight? Did it come straight at you, or—"

"Straight at us, its eyes terrible, its teeth like swords," Cech said, shaking his blond shaggy head, "and the flame . . ."

"And *where* did it come from? Can't you agree on that? Didn't you see where it went? How can I know where to search if you can't remember better than that!"

"The islands, maybe," someone said hesitantly. The men shifted closer together.

"Circled and circled the coast of Baylentha, and bellowed," little, wiry Brische said hoarsely. "Its fiery breath, if it had come any closer, would have set the woods afire."

"Stampeded the horses—took half a day to catch the horses."

"It wanted something there, in Baylentha."

Sivich was silent for some time. Then he raised his head straight up on those bulging shoulders and looked hard at the men, and his voice came grating and low. "We ride at dawn for Baylentha."

The men shrank into themselves. Cech said softly, "What do you mean to do?"

"Catch it," Sivich said.

The room was still as death. Not a man seemed to breathe. The crack of the fire made Teb jump.

"How?" someone whispered. "How would you catch such a thing?" These men were killers, but now they were afraid. Teb guessed that a great dragon is not the same as a village full of shopkeepers and children, to murder carelessly, easily. Not even the same as a king's army. For an army is made of men like themselves, while a dragon . . . a singing dragon's fierce power was well beyond even these men. Why he felt the power of the dragon so strongly within his own small body, as if he knew it well, Teb had no idea.

Well, these big sweating soldiers were no match for it. He smiled to himself, warmed with pleasure at the prospect of it eating them all, and imagined how it would be, each one devoured slowly, with crushing pain.

Then in the silent room someone repeated the question in a harsh rasping voice. "How would you catch such a creature?"

Sivich drained his mug and wiped his mouth. "With bait, man."

"Bait?"

"Bait inside a snare."

"What bait would a dragon come to? Surely . . ."

"What snare would hold such a . . . ?"

Sivich's stare silenced the speakers. The men shifted, and Teb waited, all held equally now.

"A snare made of barge chain and pine logs," Sivich said. The pines on the coast of Baylentha were tall and straight. The barge chain used in Auric was as thick as a man's leg. The men stirred again, mulling the idea over.

"And what kind of bait?" Pischen breathed.

There was silence again. Then Sivich turned and looked over the heads of his men, directly toward Teb's corner. His voice came low and cold.

"The boy will be the bait."

Teb sat very still. He could not have heard right. He forgot to breathe, was afraid to breathe. Goose bumps came on his arms, and the blood in his wrists felt like ice. What boy did Sivich mean? Every man had turned to stare at him. Half drunk, smirking, every face had gone blood-hungry. Teb's mind flailed in panic, like a moth trapped in a jar. He wanted to run, but there was nowhere to run to. The jackals edged closer as they sensed his fear. Sivich crossed the room, kicked the jackals aside, and stood over Teb with one boot on Teb's hand where he crouched, the dark leader filling his vision, his eyes boring down into him.

Sivich jerked him up by his ear so his body went hot with pain and he stumbled and choked back a cry. Sivich snatched Teb's wrist in a greasy hand and twisted his arm back. Teb turned with the arm, to ease the pain. Sivich stared at his forearm where the little birthmark shone against his pale skin. Then the dark leader dragged him across the room toward the staring men.

They crowded at once to look. Hibben of the twisted hand drew in his breath sharply. But it was only a birthmark, Teb thought. He had always had it. Why were they staring at it? It was a dark mark, no bigger than the ball of his thumb, and looked like a three-clawed animal foot.

Sivich's fingers were hard as steel. "This will trap a dragon. With bait like this we'll have us a dragon easy as trapping fox."

The men sighed and muttered. Some pushed closer to Teb, leaning over him to stare, pawing at his arm, their strong breath making him feel ill.

"How can that catch a dragon? It's only a little mark. . . ."

"What does it mean? How can . . . ?"

But others among them nodded knowingly. "Ay, that will trap a dragon—trap the singing dragon. . . ." They stared at Teb strangely.

When at last Sivich was done with Teb, he shoved him back toward the corner. Teb went quickly, sick inside himself with something unnameable.

He crouched against the stone wall, listening as Sivich described how the snare would be built, how Teb would be bound in the center of it as the rabbit is bound in the fox snare. And, Teb thought, with the same result, a bloody, painful death, the dragon's great hulk hovering over him as it tore his flesh, just as the fox tears at the rabbit.

For even a singing dragon—if in truth it was such— had to eat. No one ever said that singing dragons were different in that way from common dragons. Surely the fables about their skills as oracles were only that, fables born of their beauty and size, and of the wonder of their iridescent color. Some folks thought the dragon was a sign of man's freedom. That didn't, in Teb's mind, make it less likely to behave like other dragons when it was hungry.

Or was it something other than hunger that Sivich felt would draw the dragon to him? What was the mark on his arm? Why was it important? Yet common sense told him that the wondrous tales of the singing dragons were only myth; and certainly there was nothing magical in a small brown birthmark.

Teb was not a king's son for nothing. Wonder and

24

myth were one thing, but fact remained separate and apart. He had spent many hours in the hall listening as his father threaded a keen path between gossip and truth, in appraising the dark raiders and preparing his men for battle. But even then, his father had at last been wrong, had been misled by falsehood that looked like truth. He had believed in Sivich's loyalty, when Sivich was really a clever pawn of the dark. He had died for his misjudgment.

Why did Sivich want the dragon? What could he possibly do with it? Keep it in the trap forever? Poke it and torment it? But you couldn't keep a dragon captive, not that dragon. Why would he want to?

Because the dragon was a symbol of freedom? Must they destroy every such symbol, the dark raiders and their pawns who had helped enslave half the northern lands? Must they destroy everything loved by free men?

Yes, Teb supposed. If the dark raiders could enslave the dragon, they would show all of Tirror they held the last symbol of freedom in chains. Their power would be invincible then. No one would defy them then.

Teb went cold as a harsh voice at the back shouted, "A princess would be better bait. What about the girl— hasn't she the mark?"

"The girl has no such mark," Sivich said irritably. "Besides, I keep her for breeding."

"No one breeds a girl of fourteen," said Hibben of

the twisted hand. "They die in childbed all the time, bred young."

Sivich turned a look of cold fury on the soldier. "Do you think I'm stupid? The girl will be kept to breed when she can bear me the young I want, as many young as it will take to capture every singing dragon that ever touches Tirror's skies. She will breed male babies with the mark."

Hibben grunted, then was silent.

Teb watched Sivich. What *was* the meaning of the mark? For it was the mark, surely, that had kept Sivich from killing him as he had killed his father. He felt panic for Camery, and knew she must get away. Both of them must. But how? How could Camery escape from a tower with winged jackals circling it? The guards never let her come down.

Sivich was talking about the snare again, how many trees would be felled, how much chain was needed. Teb listened, sick to despair at his helplessness. Would old Desma help him? But she was too afraid. The only other servant he trusted was Garit, and he had been sent to the coast to gather and train fresh horses, and had taken young Lervey with him. There was no one. The hall felt icy. He crouched, shivering, and listened to the drunken talk. It was nearly dawn when at last the hall lay empty. A heavy rain started, splattering in through the barred window. Teb pressed exhausted against the stone, shivering and lost, and fell into a sick uneasy sleep.

3

"Get the boy up! Get him out here! Do you think we have all day!" Sivich's voice thundered up from the courtyard and jerked Teb from sleep. He lay struggling between consciousness and dream, and realized he had been hearing shouts and the sounds of restive horses for some time, pounding in and out of his dreams. He tried to escape back into sleep, but now the image of the dragon filled his head suddenly, the image of himself in the dragon's gaping jaws. He had gone to sleep thinking of that, and didn't know how to stop thinking it.

He reached for a blanket that wasn't there, then realized he was still in the hall. He had slept in the corner. Someone had put the ankle chain on him, chained him to a ring in the wall. The hall smelled of wet ash,

and he remembered it had rained. Rain always came down the chimney. The bars of the window were wet, and water streaked the wall and puddled on the floor. Beyond the bars, the sky was dull and heavy.

The jackals were stirring and snuffling.

A door banged suddenly, and Teb watched Blaggen come across from the scullery. He could smell eggs cooking, and ham, and could hear the din of men eating in the common room.

Blaggen pushed the jackals aside and knelt stiffly to remove Teb's chain. There was a stain of egg on his tunic, and his hair was uncombed. He dropped the chain into his pocket and stood up, took a slab of dry bread and cheese from his pocket, and handed them to Teb.

"I'm not hungry."

"Put it in your pocket, then. Could be your last meal."

Teb wadded the food in his fist and shoved it in his pocket.

Blaggen pushed him across the shadowed, echoing hall and down the steps to the courtyard, then out among the milling horses and warriors. The two jackals kept so close now that he could hardly move. When they began to sniff his pocket for the bread and cheese, slavering and growling, Teb turned his back, slipped the food out, and gulped it. He hoped it would stay down. He worked his way to the water trough, falling over the jackals, stumbling between horses and men.

He drank. The water tasted like metal. He turned away, feeling awful, pushing between two big warhorses and wondering if he was going to throw up. Then when he looked above him toward the tower, Camery was there at the window.

She stood very still, looking down at him. Her face was so white, as if the sun of Tirror never reached her; yet watery sun caught her now from low in the east, tangled in her pale hair. She was hugging herself as if she were cold. They looked at each other across that impossible distance. They could not speak. Neither could know what the other was thinking. Neither could know the fate of the other. Camery did not know, at the moment, that they would likely never see each other again. She would guess it when he rode away. And he thought, as he watched her, *I won't die! I won't!*

But their father had died. Their mother had died— neither had wanted to die or had gone to death willingly.

What would become of Camery?

He felt so sick for her. He could only look at her and look as she stared down at him. It started to rain again in hard little needles, as the warriors began to mount up.

Blaggen jerked Teb around, took him by his collar and the seat of his pants, and flung him into the saddle of a big bay gelding, then tied Teb's hands behind him and laced his feet together under the horse's belly.

29

The gelding's halter was tied to the horn of Blaggen's saddle. Blaggen mounted, and his horse snorted and lunged, jerking Teb's mount and sending him humping along behind the black's rump, nearly unseating Teb. He felt clumsy with his hands tied behind him and no reins to hold to help him know the horse's intentions and communicate his own.

All around him jackals began to crowd in among the horses and mounting men, and some of the horses snorted at them and reared. The hump-shouldered, low-bellied jackals paid no attention to the soldiers' commands, but only snarled insolently. Teb began to watch the frightened horses, for they were new and young, and unused to the winged jackals. New horses— where had they come from? He stared around at the mounted men until he spied a thatch of red beard and red hair all running together in a great mane. Garit! Garit was back. He had brought the trained colts from the coast, two- and three-year-olds, still young and skittish, but ready to be ridden. Teb watched Garit dismount in fury and lash at the jackals with a heavy strap.

Sivich shouted with anger and spurred his horse at Garit. "Put down your strap. *I* command the jackals."

"Get them away, then. They're frightening the colts."

"Settle your colts! What kind of training are they getting if they can't abide the palace guard?"

Garit took two rearing young horses by the reins, ignoring the efforts of their riders, and held them gently and firmly as he stared up at Sivich. "They are young and afraid. I will not have them ruined. They need to get used to the jackals slowly, not have the stinking things crowding them at first sight. The smell alone is enough to drive a horse mad. Get them away or I will have every colt back in the stables, and you can ride the damned jackals."

Sivich looked as if he would come right off his horse and take sword to Garit. Teb held his breath. There was a long silence as the two stared at each other. Then Sivich backed off, glowering, and motioned to Blaggen. "Send the jackals across the courtyard. Bring only three with us, to guard the boy. And keep them away from the precious babies." His voice was clipped with fury, and Teb was amazed that he had let Garit boss him.

Well, but there was no one else in Tirror who could serve as horsemaster with half the skill and knowledge of Garit. Sivich knew quite well that if he wanted reliable mounts, he could not afford to lose Garit. Sivich spat, kicked his horse around savagely as an insult to Garit, and galloped to the head of the troops. As he started out through the gate, the rain softened to a fine mist, dimming the courtyard and clinging to the horses' manes. Teb turned to look back at the tower. Camery had not moved. He wished with all his soul he could speak to her.

He wished he could have left a written message with Desma, to be hidden in Camery's food tray, but even had he had the chance, he could not read or write, could put little more than his own name to paper.

His mother had started to teach him, before she went away. He supposed she had thought Camery would continue the teaching, but neither had felt much like lessons. And then suddenly it was too late.

Had his mother meant to return to them? Her last words to them were so strange. She had talked, not about herself and her journey or if she meant to come back, but only about how it would be to be grown-up one day and have to make decisions they didn't like. She had shown them a small sphere the size of a plum, made of gold threads that wound through it crossing and recrossing in an endless and complicated trail. She had said that was what life was like, all paths crossing and linked. Teb didn't understand. She had said the sphere stood for the old civilization that once had reigned on Tirror, when all creatures, human and speaking animal, all individual beings, trod paths linked to other lives in a harmony that did not exist anymore. Teb didn't understand her words with any kind of reason, though he felt a deep sense of something true in them. She had said the sphere stood for something more, too, but did not tell them what. She said they would know one day. She had worn it on a golden chain when she went away.

As the horses moved up the hills in the rain, Teb looked back once more at the receding palace, then hunched down, shivering, and lost himself in a dream of the old days, that time his mother called the age of brightness. There had been many small busy cities then—most lay in ruins now. They had been rich with little shops and small industries. All manner of craftsmen and husbandrymen and farmers had worked happily side by side, trading back and forth in a rich and complicated bartering. His mother said it was a time when all humans and speaking animals were filled with the joy of being alive, of being themselves in some special way that Teb could grasp only as a feeling of excitement.

In that time, because of the harmony she spoke of, children could often gather the strains of a simple magic together in their crafting—to create, for instance, sails made of butterfly wings to carry a feather-light boat along the rough rivers. Or to create special places— a bedchamber woven of spider gauze and dew of new leaves. Children apprenticed as they chose, to craftsman or hunter or farmer. And if the finest in the craft was a speaking animal—which was often the case with hunting—then, of course, the child would apprentice to him and go to live among the foxes or wolves or great cats. In the mountains, the dwarfs and animals mined together for silver and gold. In the valleys of snow, the unicorns worked side by side with men to find and gather the candlemaking berries and to harvest the skeins of silk from giant snow spiders, the unicorns winding the silk on their horns so the men could spin and weave cloth.

There had been more traveling in the old times, happy journeys when craftsmen of all kinds made long, leisurely trips to exchange goods and ideas with those in other countries. Many children went on such journeys, groups of them stopping at night at the temples that stood on all the traveled routes welcoming animal and human, giving shelter.

Governing had been done by council in all the small city-nations, these coming together in larger groups when there was need to vote on issues that affected many countries. The few wars that occurred had been with the far northern peoples, wars fought bravely— speaking animals and humans side by side. His mother had said it was the northern tribes of Habek and Zembethen that had brought evil into the land, turning their good magic awry with their own greed until it produced only evil. They had changed the weather so the crops would not grow in the south; they had taken children into slavery and the speaking animals to perform in circuses. It was their greed and growing evil that had at last rent a hole in the fabric of the world, and had allowed the dark to enter. Because of the changes they had wrought, the small, individual freeholds had vanished, and many of the bigger, impersonal kingdoms were ruled by jealous despots. Now, more folk worked for others or in the service of kings, doing as they were bid rather than as they themselves chose. His mother seemed filled with anger for the loss of that earlier time and would pace sometimes when she talked of it, as if by her very energy, she could bring back some of its magic.

He remembered his mother best in the walled garden, for it was there the children could be alone with her away from her duties in the palace. She wore red often, and he could see her in his mind sitting before the bright flowers of the flame tree. They often had tea there, with seedcakes and fruit. It was here she would sometimes sing to them songs that filled them with wonder, songs that seemed more than songs, that made scenes from the past come vividly alive. After she sang, though, she was quieter and seemed sad. Sometimes she seemed to Teb as if she did not quite belong—to the palace, or even to them as a family. Her other great pleasure was when she rode out across the hills on one of Garit's new skittish colts, a pleasure she looked forward to eagerly when training began in the spring. At those times, the children's own ponies would trail behind her snorting mount as she directed, and she would seem gone in a wildness and freedom where they could never follow. Something seemed to call to her then, and when they returned to the palace, Teb's father would kiss her as if she had been away a long time, as if he saw something wild in her that was reluctant to return at all.

It had been a fall morning, very cold, when their mother rode out for the last time on her bay mare, leading a provisioned packhorse. The children had stood amazed and silent, filled with her brief good-bye. They had waited for a long, long time there at the palace gate, but she did not turn back. Then their father came to get them, locking the great iron gates in silence.

Had their mother and father quarreled? Was that what made her go away? They hadn't quarreled often, or severely. But before she left, Teb and Camery had heard the rise and fall of their voices late into the night. Whether in argument or only in grown-up talk, they could not tell.

After she went, their father was preoccupied and restless. Then months later the sheep farmer came, telling of her drowning and bringing her cape and her boot. Somehow her death seemed a twin horror now, with the threat of war increasing violently as new fighting broke out in many countries. An even greater evil seemed to take hold across Tirror, too, for returning soldiers spoke of dark warriors without expression on their faces, with only darkness reflected in their eyes, warriors they called the unliving. It was with the coming of the unliving that the last traces of magic, the small, bright remains of a once-great power, began to vanish from Tirror. The soldiers spoke of simple pleasures turning to evil, simple folk embracing evil ways. The unliving took great numbers of slaves, and their treatment of the slaves was terrifying.

The tapestries in the palace showed scenes of past wars and enslavements. The tapestries hung in the hall and private chambers, intricate pictures made of embroidered silk, once as brilliant as color could be.

They were filled with other scenes, too, besides war, scenes of the speaking animals and of places the children could only dream of. The tapestries had been their mother's dowry when she married their father. They warmed the palace both by holding real warmth against the stone walls and by warming, with their rich and intricate pictures, the mind and spirit of all who looked upon them.

After Sivich had killed Teb's father and brought new troops from the northern countries to mingle with those of the old palace guard, Sivich's warriors had defiled the tapestries, stained and torn them, knocking one another against them, spilling ale against them as they jostled, and even urinating on them. Palace windows were left unshuttered, so rain came to soak them and wind to lash them until now they were dull and ragged. This hurt Teb, because there was something of his mother there, something secret and touched with wonder.

A horse nickered, Teb's mount answered, and ahead of the troops, grazing sheep moved away at their approach. The three jackals rose, flapping, to lunge at them, but Blaggen called them back. A colt shied at the heavy flying creatures, and Blaggen sent the jackals to the rear of the troops with a shout and a lash of his whip. His horse pressed against Teb's, bruising Teb's leg. Teb turned in the saddle to look behind him, clumsy with his hands and feet tied. He watched the pack horses and servants that made up the rear of the long line. There were ten great draft horses, led by grooms and loaded with bundles of chain from the river barges, for the dragon trap. Two horses carried cross-cut saws and building tools, axes and sledges and spikes.

Down the hills on his left, to the south and west of Auric Palace, lay the roofs of the fishing and commercial towns of Bleven and Cursty and Rye, brown thatched roofs dotted between green garden patches, the harbors thick with little fishing boats and with the barges that plied the two rivers and the inland sea. Teb thought, No one there knows I am to be killed. Would anyone even care? They are all slaves to Sivich now. Sivich's warriors walk their streets and give them orders, and take the riches of trade they earn, and kill them if they don't do as they're told. They haven't any king anymore. He felt within himself a betrayal of Auric's people. His father had loved Auric's families as equals, and had always felt a duty to them, to keep the land safe, to keep it free of men like Sivich. Teb knew that if he died, he would betray that heritage. A heavy sadness rode with him, and anger stirred him as well as fear.

He listened to the *slop, slop* of hooves in the mud and shivered in his wet clothes. The trail was rising steeply, the horses moving up the highest slope of Auric's stony hills. Above rose the bare spine of raw granite that marked the border between Auric and Mithlan.

Beyond this spine they would ford two rivers—two rivers where men and horses would be floundering across, lines broken, the colts balking amid shouting and confusion. Could he find a way to escape there?

Oh, yes, he thought bitterly, why not fall off his horse, for instance? With his hands and feet tied, he could be drowned at once and escape the dragon forever. Though he could not be much wetter than he was. His clothes were soaked through, and the horse was dark from the rain that had at last moved off northward.

It was not until they had crossed the divide and forded both rivers, and were climbing again, up the steep mountain pass toward Shemmia, that Garit turned out of the mass of horses ahead and moved back along the troops, reining in his sorrel mare beside Blaggen. "Sivich wants you, Blaggen. I'll take the boy if you like."

Blaggen nodded sullenly, untied the halter rope that led to Teb's mount, and handed it to Garit. Teb remained silent and watching, surprised that Sivich would send Garit to lead him, for surely their friendship had been suspect. When Garit was sent to the coast to train the colts there, young Lervey had been sent, too, and Teb thought it was because they had all three been friends.

Now Garit's face was tight, impatient. "Listen well," he said softly, reining his mount close to Teb's. "Be ready tonight. We'll get you away if we can. Pakkna, Lervey, and I. Be ready for whatever we tell you. . . ." They could see Blaggen galloping back, scowling. Garit moved his horse away, handed the rope to Blaggen. Teb felt happier and began to look around him with interest as he imagined his escape.

The stony mountain flanked them now on their left, and several hours' ride ahead, inside that rocky ledge, lay the ruins of Nison-Serth, the old broken walls and the caves and secret pathways. Teb thought if he could escape to Nison-Serth, he could hide there nearly forever.

Nison-Serth had been a temple-shelter in the old civilization. The speaking animals had used it as much as humans had, taking shelter in their travels, coming together there for song and camaraderie, all the species and humans mingling happily. Now, though the speaking animals still existed, they kept to themselves and secret, and stayed hidden from humans. Of all the speaking animals, it was the kit foxes who had most often visited the sacred caves as they traveled across the land in their big, restless family groups.

Teb's family had picnicked in Nison-Serth sometimes, the king and queen and the children leaving the palace at dawn and galloping out, followed by old Pakkna and a pony laden with hampers and rugs. That was before the dark raiders began their attacks, before anyone thought of war.

After they had explored the caves, they would come together to picnic in the vast central cave. Its stone walls were blazoned with an immense and ancient painting that showed a fierce black unicorn, a herd of pale unicorns, and moving among them, the badgers and great cats and maned wolves, the sleek, dark otters, the winged owls, and the pale silver kit foxes. Here in the great cave Pakkna would lay out a delicious meal of roast chicken and smoked trout, fresh baked bread, and the special white cheese Auric was famous for, fruits from the orchards and hot spiced mint brew and pastries filled with honey and nuts. Teb grew ravenous, thinking of those picnics. His mother had loved the caves. She had explored deep into them, eagerly touching the ancient faded wall paintings and the carvings.

The caves of Nison-Serth were like a maze. A child could lose himself there—or hide. Teb could hardly keep from staring forward to where the stone ridge rose in a little hump that marked its entrance. But Blaggen was watching him, and he lowered his eyes and tried to look sullen and hopeless. Nison-Serth was there, though, and he would have a chance, now that Garit and Lervey were with him, and Pakkna, too. The old man was crippled and slow, but he could ride, all right.

When Blaggen moved his horse ahead of Teb's into single file, where the trail narrowed, Teb turned to look back at Pakkna.

He rode at the rear behind the servants, leading three ponies laden with bags and clanging pots. His grizzled gray beard blended against the mountain's gray stone. Teb looked at him, and Pakkna's eyes held steady and kind. He studied Teb a minute, a little frown of concern touched his brow; then a small twinkle of smile lit his gray eyes.

Teb faced forward quickly. He imagined just how he would slip out of the camp at night and rehearsed in his mind the caves and tunnels of Nison-Serth. They clustered and wound from one side of the mountain through to the far side, to come out above the Bay of Dubla. If he could make his way through the mountain, he thought he could swim the width of the bay to Fendreth-Teching. And in Fendreth-Teching surely he could find shelter. Though it was a wild land, the dwarfs and picthens who mined the rocky mountains of the Lair were not evil, only secretive and clannish. He would not like to climb high into the Lair mountains, though, if there were indeed dragons about again on the land, for the Lair was their nesting place.

He did not doubt he could escape Sivich, once Garit cut him free; he didn't dare to doubt it, or to think of failure.

4

Sivich made camp at dusk, on the wet, high meadows. Off to their left, in the west, the bare granite ridge ran away north like the backbone of a great, sleeping animal, the sun dropping low behind it. Blaggen left Teb astride the tethered horse while he unsaddled his own, then changed into dry clothes. There was a stand of saplings at one side of the meadow, and Garit and Lervey began to stretch ropes between the trees to serve as hitch rails for the horses. There were dead pitch pines, too, and one of these was dragged to the center of the meadow, the dry heart of it cut out for firewood and then set alight with oil-soaked moss.

When Blaggen was finished making himself comfortable, he untied Teb's feet and hands. "Get down. Hurry up."

Teb threw a leg over to dismount, and his hands slipped on the wet leather. He fell and landed on his backside in a shower of mud, sending the horse shying away. Blaggen snorted with laughter, then booted him and shoved him toward a small oak sapling. Here he locked the chain to Teb's leg, locked the other end around the tree, and dropped the key into his pocket.

Teb leaned shivering against the little tree, wondering if Garit could smash the lock. Or could he steal the key? The last thin rays of the setting sun touched Teb's face before it dropped behind the ridge. He could hear distant bells and could see a herd of tiny sheep grazing far down the hills, near a stone cottage the size of a doll's house, and a stream that wandered off toward Ratnisbon. If those folk down there knew he was captive, would they dare to help him? But Teb thought not; this was Mithlan, a country cowed and obedient to Sivich. It had been the first to fall to the dark raiders.

Ratnisbon was different. That country had been hard won by Sivich in desperate battle against Ebis the Black, and many of Sivich's men had died on the battlefield. Ebis had been thought killed. But he lived and he secretly brought together an army of infiltrators— servants and grooms and other innocuous townsfolk— an army that soon enough overthrew the captains Sivich had left behind and took back their land.

Would Sivich try to recapture Ratnisbon? Surely

Quazelzeg, the dark lord Sivich served, would try.

Teb had only a vague knowledge or understanding of the structure of the dark forces, but he knew they employed many pawns such as Sivich, common soldiers lured to the ways of the dark, swearing fealty to the dark rulers. He knew, from his father's words, that only by use of such ordinary, inconspicuous people could the dark forces hope to rule completely. Sivich, who had served his father's army since he was a youth, had seemed well above suspicion, doubly so because of the vehemence with which he always spoke of the dark raiders and their ways. He had seemed an adamant enemy of the dark.

The fire was blazing now, and Pakkna had laid his big metal grill across one end and was putting on strips of mutton. The great black soup kettle stood beside the blaze. The smell of cooking meat soon began to fill the air, making Teb wild with hunger. He drank from a puddle cupped in the sapling's roots, then lay back against its thin trunk. . . .

The next thing he knew, Pakkna's hand was on his shoulder, shaking him awake.

The fire had burned down, and the men were gathered around it eating. Pakkna handed Teb a plate heaped with mutton, boiled roots, and bread. Pakkna had flour on his gray beard and streaking down his dark-stained leather apron. He leaned close as he handed down the plate. "Knife under your meat. Late tonight, cut the sapling down. Take the chain off. Don't let it crash when it falls. Tie the chain to your leg." He dropped some leather thongs into Teb's lap.

"But Blaggen will hear. He—"

"He'll be very drunk by that time."

"The jackals . . ."

"Drugged. Maybe dead, I hope." Pakkna moved away. Teb watched him slicing meat on the grid. What would the old man put in Blaggen's drink? In all the drinks? He had heard of deermoss being used that way, to make men sleep. But would it work on jackals? He slipped the knife from his plate and hid it under his leg, then tied into the mutton and roots with both hands. Nothing he could remember had ever tasted so good, hot and meaty and rich. When he was finished, he sopped the gravy with his bread until his plate was clean, ate the bread, then leaned back against the oak sapling. He felt warmer now, and hopeful again.

He woke to darkness, the fire only embers, and the camp silent except for snoring. He hadn't meant to sleep, not for so long. He fumbled for the knife. Where was Blaggen? Where were the jackals? He could see nothing in the darkness. He listened for the hoof-sucking sound of a horse walking the muddy ground, for surely Sivich had set a guard. But he could hear no guard. Maybe the guard was drugged, too? Were all the men drugged? He couldn't hear the jackals' rasping snore, but sometimes they were silent as death. He took up the knife at last, turned his back on the sleeping camp, and began to cut into the tree in angled, silent strokes, pressing down.

He cut steadily until a horse snorted; then he froze and lay still. Had someone moved among the horses? Was someone watching him? The horses shifted again, and he waited. Then at last they settled, and he began to cut again, pressing harder. The tree might be only a sapling, but the green oak was tough and springy. He put all his weight on the knife. Was this all the help Garit dare give him, the knife and the drugging of the men? But Garit had said, "We'll get you away. . . ." What more do I want? Teb thought. Such help was a precious plenty, when anyone caught helping him would very likely be killed.

Should he get away from the camp on foot, or try to take a horse? He might set the whole line of horses fidgeting. He was pondering this, pressing and sawing and wincing from the blister he had made on his palm, when he heard footsteps. He dropped down, shoved the knife under him, and lay still.

The steps came closer, and he tried to breathe slowly and evenly. He could see the tall silhouette against the embers. It wasn't Garit; the man didn't walk like Garit, and he was too tall. Before the man loomed over him, Teb shut his eyes. Then a hand reached under him and felt around until it found the knife. Teb squinted to look, and could just see in the darkness the way the hand held the blade, crippled and twisted.

Hibben knelt there fingering the knife.

It was all over now. Teb felt sick and helpless. How had Hibben known?

Hibben turned, still kneeling, so the knife swung close to Teb's face as he raised it. And he began to cut at the tree.

Long, heavy strokes, swift and sure. Teb stared.

Why was Hibben helping him? Where was Garit? Was this some kind of trick?

Hibben nudged his shoulder. "Stand up. Hold the tree while I cut on through. I'll take the weight when it falls. Brace your feet."

Teb stood up and braced his shoulder against the tree, gripping the trunk against himself as tight as he could. He could feel the trunk tremble as the knife sliced and sliced, could feel the tree begin to give way. He pressed with all his strength, then he felt it ease as Hibben stood up and grasped it above him. He moved away when Hibben pushed him, and stood helpless to do more. He felt, as much as saw, the tree let down, with a whisper of leaves, onto the wet ground. He knelt at once, slipped the chain over the stump and tied it to his leg, was ready to run when Hibben pulled him up. "Come on." He pushed Teb in among the horses so he was pressed between their warm rumps. "This one, here," Hibben gave him a leg up, pressed the reins into his hands, and backed the horse out of line, then led it with his own as they moved away from the camp. Other horses moved with them, led by men Teb could not see in the darkness.

Away from the camp, they stopped to mount. Teb stared at the dark, moving shapes, trying to make out who they were. Garit? He thought so, and breathed easier. And then someone small, who could only be Lervey. They moved out at a slow, silent walk; not even the bits jingled. Teb thought they were wrapped in cloth. There was no sign of the jackals following, no heavy rushing flight at them, no irritable, coughing bark. A rider moved up beside Teb and touched his arm. He stared up into Pakkna's bearded face. Pakkna squeezed his arm, then moved on in silence. Teb thought he heard Garit whisper a command. They rode for a long time without speaking, up across the rising meadow, moving faster when they were well away from the camp. Then at last they were on drier ground beside tall boulders, and then on a rocky trail.

They had not traveled far over the rough shingle when Garit moved his horse up beside Teb. It was lighter now, for the clouds were blowing away, and the pale constellations of Mimmilette and Casscassonne shone above the ridge. Garit leaned down as if to study the gait of Teb's mount.

"Your horse has gone lame; can't you feel it? Picked up a stone, likely. Pull him up and let's have a look. Go on, Hibben. We'll catch up."

Teb and Garit dismounted as the others moved ahead, and soon stood alone as Garit lifted the gelding's near front foot.

"I didn't feel him go lame," Teb whispered.

"Shh. He's not. I wanted you alone. Now listen well. I am going to give you some instructions pretty soon, in front of the others. I don't want you to follow them."

Teb nodded, puzzled.

"What I do want you to do is this. Go to the caves of Nison-Serth as I will tell you. But go on through them, clear through and out the other side, above the Bay of Dubla. Make sure there is no one on the coast to see you, stay hidden, get down the coast and back into Auric. Stay near the shore; keep to the brush and rocks. You can get into Bleven all right, but do it at night. Go directly to the cottage of Merlther Brish on the back street. You'll know it by the big dray horses in the side yard and the pile of barrels and the smell of malt—he's the brewer. Give him this note." Garit pressed a piece of paper into Teb's hand. "He will hide you. You are to stay there, Teb. Safely hidden. You are to wait there until I can bring you an army. Merlther will do the best he can for you."

Teb stared at Garit in disbelief.

"You will retake Auric one day. I promise you. I will bring you all the armed men I can muster."

"But how can I stay there so long and not be discovered? For years, until I grow up? So close to the palace . . . just stay—with a stranger?"

"He is your subject, Teb. Merlther will take the best care of you. And there are ways of hiding someone—cellars no one has seen, passages between the houses . . ."

"I never heard of—"

"Such things can be built in four years. Auric, young prince, has taken a lesson from Ebis the Black. Auric, too, will rise again. Do you think I got myself sent down to the coast for nothing? All it took was a little judicious criticism, a little too much complaining. I know my value as horsemaster well enough to be pretty sure he wouldn't kill or imprison me, just get me out of his hair. And he did need the colts from down there. Now mount up, lad, before they get curious. I don't trust any of them, except Pakkna. But they all wanted to be free of Sivich. Maybe they're all right—time will tell me."

"But you—what will you . . . ?"

"We'll get away. When Sivich trails us, it will not be you he follows, but us. And we'll lose him all right."

"What about the jackals? Did you kill them?"

"Only one. I couldn't find the other two in the dark; they dropped down to sleep somewhere, full of deer-moss."

"How long will they sleep?"

"Eight or ten hours."

"The men, too?"

"Yes. You should be deep in the caves by that time, maybe through them."

It was not long after they joined the others that Garit called a second halt, and the riders moved close together, their horses nosing one another, as Garit gave Teb the false instructions. They had moved up behind boulders now, where sight and sound were shielded from the plain below. Starlight touched the cliffs, and now Teb could see that the sixth rider was a tall, thin soldier called Sabe, a pale, saturnine man whom Teb had never liked. Six riders and seven horses, the seventh laden with pack. Garit put a gentle hand on Teb's shoulder.

"Sivich's men will follow us as soon as they wake and see we're gone. There was no way to hide our tracks in the wet meadow. They will follow *our* trail, Teb. You must leave us now. You must go to the caves of Nison-Serth and hide there. Pakkna tells me you know the caves well."

Teb nodded.

Garit pulled at his red beard. "The plan is this. You will go on foot from here up across the rocks, where you will leave no trail. You will wait in the caves of Nison-Serth and watch the meadow and the camp from there.

"You must wait until Sivich has sent out his trackers and the two jackals after us and has himself moved on toward Baylentha. I don't think I misjudge; I think he will take the main party there, he's that eager for the dragon. He'll want the troops who trail us to kill us, all but you, and bring you there to him.

"When the meadows are clear of him, you must move down across the border to Ratnisbon at night, and seek safe sanctuary from Ebis the Black. He will be happy indeed to shelter the Prince of Auric, for he has no love for Sivich, as you well know."

Teb nodded again and swallowed. Who among this group did Garit not trust, that he must lay a false trail? Hibben? Sabe? Surely not Lervey; he was only a boy, hardly older than Teb himself.

"It will be well if we leave a clue or two for Sivich's trackers," Garit said. "We have a length of chain for Lervey to wear when we camp, to drag through the dirt, for his feet are like in size to yours. If you will take off your tunic, Teb, I have a clean one for you in my pack. Yours will carry your scent with us, for the jackals."

Teb stripped off his brown cloth tunic. It smelled pretty high, all right. He'd worn it a long time. He put on the leather one Garit offered. It was warmer and well made, though very big for him.

Garit settled his horse, which had begun to paw. "You'd best go, Teb. Climb from the saddle onto the boulders so you make no trail. Stay atop them along the ridge to the caves. Here, we've fixed you a pack. Rope, knife and some cord, food, candles and flint and a lamp. A waterskin."

Teb climbed from the back of his horse up the boulder, then reached down for the pack and waterskin and slung them over his shoulder. Garit gave his hand a parting squeeze. He stood watching as the riders turned away and faded into the night, the sound of hooves growing quickly softer, then gone.

He turned and made his way alone toward Nison-Serth.

He would be safe in Nison-Serth. He moved toward it eagerly, feeling ahead of him in the darkness where, even in the starlight, shadows could be chasms. Nison-Serth would shelter him. He thought of his mother there, how she had loved its beauty, and it seemed to him that something of his mother beckoned to him now, a power of calm protection linked with the power of the caves.

Clouds blew across the moon, so he had to go more slowly in the dark and feel ahead carefully. He fingered the pack and felt the reassuring hard curve of the candle lamp inside. He longed to light it. He could imagine carrying the thick glass chimney before him to show him the way and to warm his cold hands.

But it would be a deadly beacon to draw Sivich. Well, if he lost his way or the going got too rocky and difficult, he would sleep among the boulders and go at first light, before anyone could see him from below. He imagined the great stone entrance of Nison-Serth, its rough triangular arch of pale stone, and tried to guess how far ahead it was. It would be hard to miss. He could picture the two standing boulders inside carved with the ancient pictures of animals and birds.

Twice he heard a noise like something slipping along behind him, and went cold with the thought of the jackals.

But they were drugged; surely they were drugged. He hurried ahead, scrambling and slipping. He had to climb higher now, around a steep drop. He could not remember this part of the cliffs near to Nison-Serth. He was tempted to light the lantern, shield it with his pack. He climbed again, then found a way down, afraid he would go too high and miss the entry. Just when he thought he had missed it, there it was, towering before him in the night, a pale vaulting arch pushing at the sky. He slipped inside.

He stood staring into the darkness, touching the carved boulders for reassurance; then he moved farther in, past them, feeling out into the darkness. He was not afraid here. He thought the caves welcomed him. He yawned, very sleepy suddenly. He groped on in the darkness, feeling the walls and remembering the curves, and the way he must go, knowing he could not light the candle until he was well away from the portal.

Deeper in, there were two tunnels so narrow and low that not even a jackal could get through. He hoped he still could. He and Camery had explored there, with ropes tied around their waists, so their parents could pull them out if they got stuck. Camery had called one the crawling tunnel, because you could go on hands and knees, and the other the wriggling tunnel, where you went belly-down, pressed in by the stone. He did not look forward to that, but it would stop any jackal.

5

Teb knelt, found a candle in the pack by feel and fitted it into the lamp, then struck flint. The cave walls leaped and twisted around him in the flickering light. He clamped on the glass chimney, then pushed deeper into the grotto. But at the great cave he paused. He knew he must stop here, must see the painted animals.

He shone his light in and saw them leap up as if they had just sprung to life, the rearing black unicorn seeming to paw and turn, the pale foxes to slip deeper into the stone. Even in the paintings, the animals' intelligence showed clearly. The way they held themselves, their expressions, showed they were quite aware of their places in time, in the world, and in the scheme of life. The sentient, speaking animals were aware of death, too, his mother had said, and so were capable of understanding the meaning of all life. The ordinary animals, living only for the moment, did not deal with such meanings, and knew death only at the instant it struck them.

Teb thought he would like to sleep in here, among the pictures of these knowing creatures. But he went on. He turned from the great cave reluctantly, robing the animals in darkness once more, and went quickly, deeper in, toward the crawling tunnel. When he reached it he tied the pack and waterskin to rope, and tied that around his waist so they would drag behind him. He went into the low hole on his hands and knees, pushing the lamp ahead.

Crawl and push, crawl and push, the lamp a yellow pool drawing him on. He thought of the other children who had crawled here, generations gone, before there was need to flee from soldiers, children playing tag with the foxes. He was through at last and pushing past a row of small den caves; then his light found the mouth of the wriggling tunnel. How small it looked, so very low.

He lay down full length, pushed the lamp ahead, and slid in. It was tight. He had grown. He wriggled and pushed, and dragged himself ahead, the walls pressing in. He could get stuck here. He could panic as Camery had panicked once.

He was soon very hot and uncomfortably thirsty. He could not reach behind him for the waterskin. He pushed deeper; the stone pressed his shoulders and arms. He began to sweat under the weight of the stone. He wanted to thrust it away, pushing at it with his elbows, sweating harder, his heart pounding; then at last he lay still.

But he must go on. The middle was the smallest; it couldn't be much farther. He inched forward, squeezing, his clothes catching on the stone. So hot, the walls pressing in and in . . . Sweat ran down inside the heavy leather tunic and matted his hair. He pushed ahead an inch, another inch. Why had he come this far? He could never back up, never. He was trapped here. He wanted to scream out and pound with his fists but could hardly move his arms.

Then suddenly his outstretched hands felt the walls give way, felt only space as the tunnel ended; and with one final, straining shove, he shot out into the free, open cave.

He stood up, sucking in air, then stretched tall. He untied the pack and waterskin and drank, then stripped off the hot tunic. He pulled off his boots and pants, working them free of the chain. He stood naked and free, and only then able to breathe again, fully.

Then very carefully, to see if he could, he slid into the tunnel again, feet first, slipped back a little way, then out again. Yes, it was easier naked. Scratchy, though. But he knew he could get back all right, with his clothes off. He took up the light and followed it into the first of the small den caves. Here he drank again, then began to shiver in the cave's chill. He pulled on his clothes and lay down with his head on the pack. It was then he remembered Garit's note and pulled it from his pocket. He held it close to the flame, but the words were only rows of marks. He picked out his own name, nothing more. What if his life were to depend on his ability to read such a message?

He was nearly asleep when he thought he should blow out the candle, but knew he could not sleep in the pitch dark that night, even if fire ate air. Besides, there were small open portals in the caves higher up, and all these caves were connected. He turned over, sprawling on the cold stone floor, and gave in at last to sleep.

He did not know he was watched, and had been watched since well before he climbed off his horse onto the boulders.

When they were sure the boy slept deeply, the foxes slipped into the cave, wary only of the burning lamp, and stood watching him and drinking in his scent. Twelve pale foxes.

They had started following Garit's band when first the six riders came up off the meadow onto the stony ridge, followed and observed and listened. They knew everything Garit had said, both to the group and to Teb alone. They understood quite well who Teb was, son of the King of Auric, but to make sure they crowded close, now, around him and nosed softly at his arm until, in sleep, he turned it, so they could see the mark.

It was there, yes. The mark of the dragon. They were pleased, and awed.

"He is shivering," said Pixen. "He has no fur to warm him."

The foxes stared at Pixen, then began to turn around in little circles, close to Teb. They lay down, one then another, close all around him and over him, across his legs, his stomach, his chest, their bushy tails curled around him. And so they warmed him. One vixen, small and young, nuzzled her nose into the hollow of his neck. Soon he slept quietly, sprawled and abandoned in pure warmth. They sniffed at him with their thin foxy noses and watched him with humor and curiosity, then slept themselves, lightly, alert for noises in the tunnels, guarding as well as warming the prince. But then near dawn they all slipped away, and he was quite alone when he woke.

He had no notion how long he had slept or what time of day it might be. It was absolutely dark, for the candle had burned down and gone out. He fumbled in the pack for another, all the time frowning and trying to remember something. A dream? A warm dream, wonderfully cozy, as he used to feel when he was small and his mother cuddled him. But what the dream had been, exactly, he could not remember.

He thought the cave smelled different, a pungent, sharp scent. Was there some creature in here with him? He struck flint and lit the candle quickly. But the cave was empty. He dug out the old candle butt and placed the new one in the holder.

He made a meal of cold mutton and boiled roots. There was also jerky in the pack, and bread and cheese. And eight more candles, he saw with relief. He mustn't burn one tonight though—he must make everything last as long as he could. I will be out by tonight, he thought, on the coast. He could almost smell the salt of the bay. He felt rested now and eager to get on.

He would have to go back through the narrow tunnels, start at the great cave, and go through the hall of pillars in order to get to the western gate. But first he would go to the high caves and have a look at Sivich's camp. It seemed much longer than one night since he had sat chained to the oak sapling and drunk from its roots. Where were Garit and Pakkna now? Had they gotten away? Were Sivich's men following them? Or had they come to the caves?

He did up the pack, shouldered it, slung on the waterskin, then left the little cave to find the spiral tunnel that led to the upper caves. The walls were not carved here but rough, of a reddish stone and wet where springs leaked down, reflecting the lamplight.

When he stood at last in the highest cave, looking out its thin slit of window, the sun hung half up the eastern sky, at midmorning. Below and to the north lay the site of Sivich's camp, empty now, the circle of grass darker where it had been trampled into the wet earth, a black scar in the center where the campfire had burned. Three dark thin lines led away, the tracery of muddied trails across the clear green grass. One was their own trail, going off toward the ridge. A second followed beside it, as if the trackers had kept the first trail clear, for the jackals to scent along.

The widest trail led away north toward Baylentha, just as Garit had expected. As Teb stood watching the land, he heard a soft noise behind him in the passage, and whirled to look. He saw nothing. Maybe rats, he thought. It came again, a brushing sound very like the wings of a jackal.

He slipped the knife out of the pack and backed into a shadowed corner where the light from the slit window was dimmest. He watched the twisting corridor and the cluster of small arches for a long time, but nothing moved there, and the sound did not come again. Probably only rats. Jackals would already have attacked.

Then when he returned to the wriggling tunnel at last, to make his way back toward the entry and the great cave, his nerve failed him. If he were trapped in there by the jackals attacking from behind him or at his face, there would be no way to fight them.

But they couldn't have come through; it was too narrow for them.

He took off his clothes and stowed them in the pack, tied the chain tightly around his leg, tied pack and waterskin to the cord and the other end around his waist. Then, knife in one hand and lamp in the other, he lay down and slid into the tunnel.

He wriggled through faster this time. Soon he was out of it, the ordeal behind him, and no sight or sound of the jackals. Only the crawling tunnel remained ahead, and already he could see daylight filtering in. He dressed and went on.

He reached the great cave again, and again held his lamp up. There was power here that drew him, and again in the flicking light all the animals seemed to come alive, the unicorn and foxes, the great wolves and the big cats, the badger hermits and the winging owls and the laughing, gamboling otters. He had no notion how long he had stood looking when he heard again a small shuffling, then a stone dislodged behind him somewhere near Nison-Serth's entrance. He spun just in time to catch the flash of a small pale shape vanishing beyond the cave door.

It was too small to frighten him, but far bigger than any rat. He followed it, skirting the tall boulders that made the passage wall, then stood staring down the passage and into the four caves he could see. Nothing moved. He started to turn away, and then quite suddenly there were pale creatures all around him come out of the caves like magic, come out of the shadows—foxes, kit foxes crowding all around him, standing on their hind legs to touch him and stare at him. "Tebriel," they barked. "You are Tebriel." He fell to his knees and put out his arms, and they crowded close—pale silver foxes, their faces narrow and jaunty and sly, their sharp little mouths open with laughter, their bushy tails waving, a dozen kit foxes as innocent and laughing and welcome as anything a boy could have dreamed. "We welcome you, Tebriel, Tebriel of Auric," barked the largest dog fox, who surely was their leader. He nuzzled Teb, and stood laughing.

"Yes, I am Tebriel. How did you know?" He hugged and petted them. They were warm and sleek, silky and soft. They licked his face and hands, their teeth as white as new snow, their dark eyes so filled with merriment that Teb laughed out loud and drank in their sharp, foxy smell.

While he crouched there with them, laughing with them for no reason and for every reason, for the sheer delight of their meeting, another fox appeared alone at the portal, a silhouette against the morning sky, a lone sentinel. She yapped once, then ran to them.

"The riders come along the ridge," she panted. "They have *jackals*! Stinking *jackals*!" She went directly to sit before the big dog fox. "The riders follow the boy, as you said they would, Pixen."

Pixen reared and stood looking around him. "Quickly, into the tunnel of pillars, into the southern den."

The foxes leaped and pushed at Teb. He ran with them, the light from his lantern swinging in arcs along the cave walls until Pixen barked, "Put the light out." Teb stopped and blew out the candle. He could see

64

nothing, and was propelled ahead, stumbling, by the foxes pressing and urging him on.

"Left!" Pixen cried. "Left, and duck. Crawl through, Tebriel, quickly. Squeeze through; it's not far."

He did as he was told, crouched, then found he must go on his belly. He pushed pack and lamp and water-skin in first, could feel the foxes behind him pressing him on. The stone scraped his back, and he thought he would be terrified again; then, as suddenly as it had started, the crawl was ended.

"Stand up, Tebriel. You can stand. But do not light the lamp. We will lead you."

The foxes pressed against his legs and pushed him forward like a tide. Though Pixen said he could walk upright, he kept feeling above him for the cave's roof, for the way was narrow and close, a long, twisting way before the cave began to grow lighter. Then they pushed through a small arch, with light ahead of them, and stood in the huge, light, echoing hall of pillars, though they had come by a different route from the one Teb knew. Pointed pillars of stone grew from the ceiling and from the floor, awash in light from the slitted windows along a high ledge.

"We are safe," Pixen said. "They can't get in—the larger entry is blocked with boulders, has been for nearly a year. Sivich will not find us here."

"How did you know about Sivich? How did you know my name?"

"Everyone knows about Sivich, and about Quazelzeg

and his plans for Tirror. And as for you, Tebriel, we knew you by your scent.

"You and the queen and king, and Camery, used to picnic in the caves. We watched you often from the shadows, and followed when you explored.

"Last night when your little band of six passed close to us in the dark, we knew your scent, and Pakkna's scent, and we followed you.

"We heard Garit's instructions. Both sets of them," Pixen said, grinning.

"Why didn't you speak to us, when we came on picnics?"

"We saw no need to. We thought it best to remain . . . shy." Pixen turned from Teb and began to pace, his bushy tail flicking with heavy grace each time he turned. His shining coat was the color of wood ashes, very long and thick, with little silver guard hairs mixed in. His throat and chest were snowy white. The insides of his ears, when he stood against the light, shone pale pink. The only dark thing about him was his eyes—they were almost black and filled with a devilish, challenging, and complicated gleam.

"Even if we had not recognized your scent, Tebriel, there would still be the mark to tell us."

"You have sharp eyes. And what . . . ?"

"We saw the mark last night," Pixen interrupted. "While you slept."

Teb stared.

Pixen was filled with laughter. "Were you cold last night, Tebriel? Did you sleep soundly?"

"I don't think I was cold. No, I was so tired . . ." Teb paused. "No, not cold at all. Warm. I was . . ." Then he realized that it was their strong foxy scent that he had smelled in the cave when he woke. He stared at the foxes, for they were all laughing now. "It was you there! All of you—keeping me warm last night!" Now he could remember very well the feel of warm fur covering him, and he was laughing, too. "But why did you go away?" That only made them laugh harder, a soft, yapping laughter.

"Now," said Pixen at last, "you must tell us the rest of the story. There is much we do not understand. If we are to help you, we must know what the trouble is about."

"It—it started with the birthmark," Teb said. "Well, with the dragon, really."

"The dragon?" the foxes breathed, looking at him with wonder. "What kind of dragon?" said one. "*Is* there a dragon?" said another. The foxes gathered around him just as he and Camery used to settle to hear their mother tell a tale.

As he told them about the night in the hall when Sivich learned of the dragon, and how Sivich meant to snare it, their expressions grew serious, then angry, and Pixen said, "The dark raiders must be stopped. The dragon must not be harmed; no trap must touch the goddess, and there is little time."

"The goddess?" Teb said.

"The dragon they saw is female," Pixen said. "By her color, she is female. The male is dark. She is a goddess, Teb, to us all."

"But goddesses aren't . . . They're just in stories. Folk don't believe in—"

"We call her goddess," Pixen said, "even though she is mortal. The dragons guarded the freedom of the old times, Tebriel. Through their songs, they helped folk relive the lives of their ancestors. When a dragon and bard came into a city, crowds would gather to hear them. Their songs made Time seem like a river, carrying scenes bright with the lives of those who had lived before. It was by dragon magic that one knew how wars had been fought, and men conquered and then freed. It was by dragonsong that folk were helped to understand the nature of evil, and so to understand goodness, too. But you . . ." The kit fox broke off, and studied Teb. "What is your age, Tebriel?"

"I am twelve."

"And you have been alone for four years?"

"My mother has been dead for five years. My father the king for four. Sivich murdered him. Camery— Camery is captive, in the tower."

"And you have lived as the slave of Sivich?"

Teb nodded.

"And your mother told you nothing of the dragons? Nor did your father?"

"I—my mother said they were filled with wonder

and power. She thought there weren't any singing dragons left on Tirror, and that made her angry and . . . I don't know. Sad, I guess."

"She told you nothing more?"

"No. She—"

But Pixen had turned away as a noise and stirring at the entrance distracted them all, and two foxes leaped in through the tunnel.

"They have come into Nison-Serth," said the smaller, a young vixen. "The jackals are *horrible*. Nosing everywhere and snuffling, and flapping . . . *disgusting*."

"I want four messengers," Pixen said, "to go quickly down into Ratnisbon, to Ebis the Black, to carry a message for his ears alone. Mixet, Brux, Faxel . . . and yes, you may go, Luex. I would not send Faxel without you. Now come, let me give you the message.

"You are to tell Ebis the Black that Sivich builds a huge trap on the coast of Baylentha, to capture the singing dragon. You will tell him that Sivich means either to hold her captive or to kill her. Sivich must be stopped, and Ebis is the only one who can stop him. You will not say you have seen Tebriel or know where—" He stopped speaking and cocked his ears. They all could hear it. Hoofbeats above their heads, across stone, as searchers rode over the great stone spine of the mountain.

6

Pixen finished his instructions, and the four foxes slipped away while the hoofbeats still pounded overhead across the mountain.

"Sivich's riders," Pixen said. "Heading for the west portal."

Teb shivered. "They'll come in there, too; they'll be all over the caves."

"They won't get in here," Pixen repeated.

"But can't they look in through the slits? Can't they see us?"

"No man can climb that sheer wall. The slits were meant for arrows once, during the five wars, long-seeking arrows trained on the sea path below, and they could not be reached by invaders. Now they are only for light and air, but still no man can climb to them."

"Then—then they'll wait at both portals," Teb said, beginning to feel hopeless. "Wait for me to come out."

"There is another way out. A way no soldier knows." Pixen paused to scratch the side of his long, thin face against his leg. Then he looked up at Teb with a bright gleam of mischief. "You are small—you can manage the fox burrow to the south. It comes out far below the west portal and is well hidden among tumbled boulders and brush. Now it is time for rest, Tebriel, for we will travel before evening." Pixen curled down and wrapped his tail around himself, and settled his nose against his tail.

Teb tried to rest, but he was nervous with apprehension and thought he could still hear hooves. He made a meal of bread and cheese, and sat watching the slits above. The cave grew brighter and warmer as the sun dropped past noon and shone in. Once he heard men just beyond the cave entrance, heard the shuffle of boots and voices muttering. Twice he heard the jackals come to the hole, snuffling and growling. The fox guards sat steady, watching the hole, knowing the jackals couldn't get through. These jackals were not like the jackals of the far north, who resembled small wolves. It was no wonder the foxes found their low-bellied, hump-shouldered presence repugnant. Compared with those of the delicate foxes, their broad flat heads and mouths like steel traps were crude and disgusting. Teb held his knife ready, almost wishing he could attack one of them, and was still holding it when Pixen woke. The fox leader stared at it and grinned.

"That steel blade, together with a fox's ripping teeth, ought to do those belly-draggers in." He yawned and shook himself. "But your scent and ours are all over the caves, Tebriel. I don't think the creatures have sense enough to know which is freshest, even when they come so near."

They set out in early afternoon, Teb and Pixen and the seven strong young foxes, to follow the winding passages inside Nison-Serth south to the fox warren. At first the passages were stone; then they turned to earth. Teb went on his belly and began to feel like a mole. But he was not afraid now, with the foxes to help if he got stuck, and by dusk they were in the warrens. They stood in a central gallery with caves opening off in all directions.

"The warren is new," Pixen said, "compared to Nison-Serth. Only a few generations have used it. We had no need of dens in the old days, when men and animals shared Tirror equally, for then we were wanderers, and we made the sanctuaries like Nison-Serth and Mund-Ardref and Gardel-Cloor our bases. But now, with the dark raiders on the land, we have taken to staying where we have shelter to hide and raise our cubs. It is not a carefree life, but safer.

"Once, when the first warren caves were opened and dug out deeper and larger, there were humans often in Nison-Serth. When the first wars began to enslave, humans helped us to dig and clear the caves of fallen stone. The children would crawl into the smaller caves, to dig there—so many children. . . .

"But come, Tebriel, my den is just here, and Renata will be waiting."

Pixen led Teb on through a small ragged opening, then down seven turnings. The low twisting passage grew lighter; then there was brightness ahead. They came into a brightly lighted cave with high ceilings and slits along the top letting in the rays of the sun. Teb could see ferns through the holes and knew the hilltop was there. At the back of the den a waterfall splashed down, frothing over the pale walls, into a deep pool stained green by the ferns that grew around it. And all around the den, the pale, nearly white walls were carved with the pictures of foxes, and of owls and all the speaking animals, as well as deer and rabbits and mice, and with strange signs that Teb could not make out.

He thought at first that humans must have done the carving, but then he began to see that each line was made of three parallel lines such as might be made by claws.

"The stone is soft," Pixen said, watching him. "Limestone. Five generations of my family have carved their dreams into these walls."

"They are beautiful." But they were more than beautiful; they were powerful carvings that lifted Teb and made him think of strange half dreams and grasp at thoughts that eluded him, filled him with desires that he could not sort out. He wanted to look and look, but then a high whimpering sound startled him.

Opposite the pool against the far wall was a large niche where four fox cubs were waking on a pile of rabbit skins. Renata sat beside them, watching Teb with bright, curious eyes.

Renata was smaller than Pixen, and so pale a silver she was almost white, so her eyes looked huge and black in her thin little face. Her chest and throat were snow white, like her four feet, and her ears were rimmed with a line of dark gray. Dark gray marked the tip of her silvery tail. She rose and came to Teb and stood up on her hind legs to greet him, touched his hand with her paw. He put out his arm so she could rest her paws there, and she stood looking up into his eyes, sniffing his scent delicately, quietly studying his face.

"You are Tebriel. You have grown so tall. The first time I saw you, you were only a baby in the arms of your mother. . . . I am so sorry about your mother, and your father, Tebriel.

"But come, you must be tired. All that crawling and hunching. Will you rest?"

"No, but I'd like to wash," Teb said, looking with longing at the pool.

The two foxes left him, and he stripped down and jumped in, shocking himself with the cold. But in a few minutes he was tingling warm. He scrubbed and splashed and was so enjoying himself he didn't see the cubs until they were all around the pool, patting and slapping at the water, yipping and laughing at him. Then the bravest one dove in and had a fine swim, and by the time Pixen and Renata returned, Teb had dried himself and the cubs on the soft rabbit skin Renata had left him. The cubs were asleep again in a tangle near the pool, underneath the ferns. Renata licked them lightly, then touched Teb's hand with her nose.

"Would you like to see the rest of the den?"

She led him behind the sleeping alcove and through a small arch, and they were in a dim corridor with six small caves opening from it. "Two are escape entrances," she said. "They lead to other clusters of dens and out a secret way."

There were two storage dens for food. In one, little carcasses of rabbits and mice and squirrels, none of them speaking animals, had been laid to dry, and there were mounds of hazelnuts. In the other were stores of blueberries and bayberries and sweet nettle leaves, and heaps of dried mushrooms and wild apples and plums. Beyond these rooms was a room for curing hides, and then a latrine room, with a pit that could be covered with earth, and another dug. When they returned to the central cave, the cubs were awake and playing again. They raced at Teb and circled him, yapping sharply, nipping at his legs and toes. He knelt and gathered them in, furry and squirming, and in their delight they toppled him so he lay sprawled with them on top.

Renata drove them off, scolding, and they sat in a row, obedient to her but with sly little grins on their faces. "Go play in the common," she said at last, shaking her head at them. And then they were gone, flicking their tails. "Now come, Tebriel, we will make a meal, and then we will take you on through the warrens, to the secret portal."

She lowered her glance and nosed the chain on his leg. "There is no way we can help you with that. It must be terrible to have a chain on your leg."

"It's better than two chains, the way they did it in my cell. If—when I get to Bleven, to the cottage of Merlther Brish, I expect he can get it off."

There were apples and plums and hazelnuts for supper, blueberries and nettle leaves, and a dried pheasant. Teb added his bread and cheese and the rest of the mutton, and the foxes enjoyed the new foods as much as Teb enjoyed the fresh fruits, which he had seen little of in the palace.

"Will Merlther Brish take good care of you, Tebriel?" Renata's ears were back, as if she would challenge poor Merlther to do just that. "Will he feed you well, and . . . will he love you?"

"I expect he will feed me well. And hide me. I don't know about the love, though," Teb said, embarrassed. "I think I would settle for just being safe from Sivich for a while."

Renata laid her head against Teb's arm. "It is ugly not to be loved. Your mother loved you very much, as did your father." Then she looked up at him. "And what of Camery? Where is your sister, Camery?"

"She is in the tower, and captive," Teb said, and before he knew it he was telling her about the talk in the hall, all about the sighting of the dragon, though, of course, Pixen had heard it all before, and how Sivich meant to use him as bait to trap the dragon and meant to use Camery to breed children. "Because of the mark," he said. "Only I don't understand about the mark. I don't understand why it is important."

Renata looked at him for a long time without saying anything. Then all she said was, "You should keep the mark covered, Tebriel. It might help to save you from Quazelzeg."

"Who *is* Quazelzeg? Why does he seek to enslave all of Tirror?"

"He is the unliving," said Pixen.

"The dead . . . ?" Teb began.

"No, Tebriel. Not the dead. The unliving. There is a vast difference."

Teb waited, not understanding.

"Death, Tebriel," said Renata softly, "is not a condition. It is not a permanent state. It is merely a passing through. A journey into another world, and into another self. Death is not an ending.

"Don't you remember, when you were small, feeling that there was something you'd forgotten? Something you almost knew, almost remembered—then it was gone?"

"I still do that," Teb said.

"So it will be in the life after this one. Fragments of this life and of all other lives will come to you unclearly—for all are linked, Tebriel. You take from one into the next, though you don't remember.

"But to be unliving is very different. It is not like the crossing-over experience of death. It is, precisely, *no* experience. Precisely *un*living. The unliving embrace and feed on the opposite to everything we find warm and joyous and filled with life. They feed on nothingness, on all that turns from life. They hate folk who go about their own pursuits with vigor and joy; they hate the strength one feels in self. They want all creatures massed in sameness, and enslaved. They hate the deep linking of one person's life with another, the linking of generations, the tales of one's childhood and one's parent's childhood, the memories that link a family, a nation, and so link all of us. Let me show you. . . ."

The vixen looked deep into Teb's eyes, and her pale silver face seemed to grow lighter still and her dark eyes larger until Teb could see nothing else, until he swam in that bright darkness. "Remember your mother, Tebriel. See her . . . see her . . . Remember your father, your sister. Remember their faces, their voices, and the things you did together. Remember it all. . . ."

The memories came flooding, a hundred memories surrounding him. They were galloping over green hills, the four of them, Camery's pale hair flying, their mother

laughing as her horse plunged up a steep hillside. Then
they were at supper in their quiet private chambers,
their father was carving roast lamb, the room filled
with its sweet gamy scent, and there was a white
tureen brimming with onions and mushrooms. His
mother wore a pale yellow dress, and was laughing.
All the memories came flooding: being tucked into his
bed, his first pony, Camery sewing a quilt, his mother's
garden, Camery's owl. . . .

And then suddenly the memories vanished. He caught
his breath. There was only emptiness.

There was nothing.

He could not remember how his mother looked, could
not remember the color of her hair, how his father
looked. . . . There was a girl. . . .

His mind was gray and empty.

The only link he had with himself or anything real
was a pair of dark huge eyes in a pale face—what was
this creature? Why was he here . . . ?

"Who am I?

"My name—I don't know my name. . . ." He was
shaking. . . .

Then suddenly the world popped back to fill his mind
bright and loud . . . alive—alive. . . . The tales of his
father's childhood in Auric, running on the sandy
shore . . . the tales his mother told him, his own memories—all of it thronging and churning in his mind
singing and alive. . . .

The little silver vixen was there before him, her dark

eyes watching him with concern. "And so, Tebriel, you have seen as the unliving would have it. They would destroy your memory and knowledge, and so destroy your self.

"So is Quazelzeg," she said. "He is the unliving. And he would make slaves of us all."

They did not leave the cave until nearly nightfall, and again Teb followed blindly as the foxes made their way through the low, narrow tunnels. Renata left an old aunt with the cubs; and three more foxes joined them at the common, so now they were twelve again as they wound and dropped and climbed through the pitch-black holes. Then at last a faint smear of moonlight far ahead, and a smell of the sea, told Teb they were coming to the western portal.

At the portal they listened, but there was no sound except the far lapping of the water. The moon was thin and its shadows indistinct. Pixen sent a young fox out to look, and he was gone a long time, returning at last with an uneasy frown.

"No strange scents, nothing stirring. The land seems empty, but I *feel* something amiss, all the same."

"Come back inside," Pixen said, and he went out himself to have a look.

Pixen was gone even longer. He returned with his ears back and his tail lashing. "There are still troops at the western portal—nine that I counted—and they have the two jackals with them. Luex was surely right, they do stink. The troops are growing restive—I think we'd better go on before they decide to explore."

Teb took up his pack and waterskin, touched the knife at his belt, and followed Pixen out the small hole, with the others crowding behind him. The bushy cover outside scratched his face and caught at his clothes, and he could not seem to go silently as the foxes did. Soon Pixen stopped. "Take off the pack and waterskin, Teb. Reeav and Mux will drag them back inside."

Rid of his belongings, Teb was able to move more quietly. He feared for the foxes, though, for even in the thin moonlight they could be easily seen. The tops of the bushes caught light, and the tops of the stones, and when they drew near to the bay, a thin path of light fell across the water. On the other side of the water rose the dark towering mass of Fendreth-Teching, topped by the rocky peaks of the dragon lair.

The little band moved along beneath a mass of bushes, Teb crawling through the leafy tunnel of branches that insisted on snagging his clothes. The foxes slipped through quite untouched. Teb breathed in the scent of the bay, salt and wild. When they came out of the bushes they were on a sheer cliff high above the water, and now the way was rocky and precarious. The foxes skipped along it and, Teb suspected, would have traveled much faster without him. He tried to see where he was by the shape and width of the bay directly below. Yes, here the bay had begun to narrow, but he could not yet see, off ahead, the thin channel linking the Bay of Dubla with the outer, seaward Bay of Fendreth. Once they reached the channel, Bleven would lie less than a mile beyond. He would go on alone then.

But suddenly heavy flapping filled the sky, and a coughing growl. The jackals were on them, dropping and snarling. Hoofbeats were pounding behind, loud on the stone as if they had just come up from softer ground.

"Run!" Pixen cried to Teb. "We'll delay them."

But Teb could not; his knife was slashing at a jackal even before he knew he had drawn it, for the creature had little Reeav in its mouth, shaking her. He slashed at its throat, then its face, but it would not let her loose. At last, with three foxes at its throat, it twisted in agony and let her go. Reeav staggered away. Mux tried to get to her, but the riders were all over them, all was confusion. A jackal grabbed Teb's leg, tearing; then he felt himself snatched up by the shoulder as a horse shied against him and he was lifted and thrown across a saddle, facedown, so the saddle back jammed hard into his ribs and belly, knocking out his breath and searing him with pain. The horse swerved, and Teb revived enough to bite the rider's arm and kick at him; he got a blow across his back that shoved him into the saddle again and made him go dizzy with pain. Then the horse was whipped to a gallop, and the pain was like fire in his middle.

———

The soldiers moved northward all night. Teb hurt so badly he wished he would die, and much of the time he was unconscious. He threw up twice, and the retching made searing stabs of pain. He didn't know when they stopped, knew nothing very clearly until he woke the next day in broad daylight with someone shoving a waterskin at him.

He lay trying to understand where he was and why he hurt, and was not clear about anything. He was in some kind of a building made with logs set wide apart so sky and seashore shone between them. The logs were lashed together with chain. The thing was like a huge cage, and he was chained inside it.

He was in the dragon trap.

He pawed at the waterskin and turned to lift it, sending fire through his middle. He soon found he could lift no weight without pain. He managed to slide closer to it and drag it up on his chest, above the hurt, and sucked at it, spilling a good deal over himself, but satisfying his thirst at last.

He lay there all day, asleep, awake, then late in the day burning one minute and shivering the next. Someone brought him food, fried rabbit and hard bread, but he was too sick to eat. He begged for a blanket and was ashamed of begging. He slept and woke, and was conscious of little, until he woke and saw it was dark. Or nearly so, for the moon was there overhead, thin and bright—and then gone. The moon suddenly gone.

He thought it was his illness making him blind. But no, there was something—something there in the night, covering the moon. Something . . .

Then he could see the moon again, but the something was still there hovering in the sky low over the cage, reflecting moonlight on its pale silvery body that stretched out long and curving, on its immense wings that shimmered across his vision far broader than the width of the cage. He stared up at her, trembling. Immense she was, and wondrous, and though he should have been terrified, should have cringed away, knowing she could kill him, he was not afraid. He was filled only with wonder, with awe and with a longing he had never known and could not challenge or question. There was no fear. Only a strange, throat-tightening love that left him confused and shaking. She lifted away higher and grew smaller, passed across the moon again, then disappeared.

And still he trembled and stared at the night and could not sleep anymore. Long after the dragon departed, she still filled his mind, her gleaming wings and her huge, clear green eyes looking and looking at him.

7

The dragon had awakened not many days before, in the mud of Tendreth Slew. She had been asleep for many years there, and she was the only singing dragon among the dozens of squat hydrus and common dragons that used the slew for concealment. When she woke and lifted her head from the muck to look around her, she saw no other like herself. She stretched her long neck up to look more carefully, and rivers of mud ran off her silvery scales. She blew from her nostrils in a shower of mud. Then she stood up with a sucking noise, and mud poured back into the hole she left. The other creatures stirred and moved away to give her room, so the whole slew writhed with their slithering.

She stared up into the dawn sky and opened her

great red maw, and roared at sky and mountains and at the world in total. The mountains thundered her call in receding echoes. She pulled one clawed foot from the mire to paw at the chill air; then she climbed out of the slew onto the stone ledge beside it with a sucking pull and made her way along the escarpment until she reached a clear, fast spring flowing down out of the mountain and into the rock-edged lake. She slid in and swam, washing herself, rolling and blowing in the deep icy water, twisting down into the depths, then up again to break surface with sprays of foam.

She came out glistening, as pale and iridescent as a sea opal. She was no color and all colors, for her glinting sides reflected the colors around her: her belly coppery from the stone beneath her, her sides brown and green from the mountain, and her back mirroring the pale dawn sky just as her dragon's mind mirrored the long, rich life of Tirror.

She stretched to dry herself, streaming water. She spread her wings on the wind and shook them so they shattered the light. She was as long as twelve horses, and slender, with a fork at the end of her tail, and two gleaming horns on her forehead. Her sharp fangs marched in two rows beside a forked tongue red as blood. Her eyes were green, though they could look azure or indigo, depending on her temper. She stared into the clouds above her, her mind filled with a thousand pictures, and she wanted to sing. But she would not sing here, alone. And then slowly she realized why she had waked. She felt the changes in her body, subtle as song itself and as compelling.

Her eggs were forming. Soon she must fertilize them. She felt the urgency to breed like a great tide, and she cried out a ringing call. Her eyes flashed, her body towered, rearing. Then suddenly she leaped skyward in an explosion of beating wings.

And if before she had been beautiful as she reflected the lake's waters, now in flight she was like jewels of ice. She lifted on the thermals and spiraled upward, bellowing her clear call, filled with the sky's freedom and with the thrill of her own power, and she headed north toward the highest, wildest peaks of Tirror to begin her search for a mate.

But was there any male left in Tirror? Had all the singing dragons but herself fled through the twisting ways into other worlds? Was she the last, all alone?

Then as she headed north she spied the army camped on Baylentha's shore, and she dropped to look. But the soldiers did not cheer her as men of old would have done, before she went to sleep. These men cowered from her and brandished weapons, and that angered her. She dove at them, bellowing, and they ducked away and cried out, and some shot arrows at her. She dove at them, spitting flame, and drove away their horses, and left them huddled together as she swept away to more urgent business.

But something about the camp on Baylentha's shore made her curious, and she returned several days later.

Now the shore was bare, so she circled and left, but still she was drawn to it, and the next time she came the soldiers were back, and now they were cutting trees and constructing something huge on the shore. They stood watching her this time with some strange urgency until she swept up away into the clouds.

Her curiosity drew her back again and again. She spent her days searching the mountains for a mate, then came to Baylentha late in the night, while the soldiers slept. Soon she knew what it was they built, and then one night there was bait in the trap, and she dropped low to see.

A young boy was tied in there. She hovered over the cage, staring at him. He slept so deeply. She rose quickly against the moon, excited because he was there, and unsettled.

The next day a male dragon began trailing her; she discovered his scent on the crosswinds, and her own inner pulses quickened; and they began the slow, elusive game of seeking that dragons desire. She should not have returned to the boy. But something insistent drew her back each nightfall.

He was always asleep when she came, and she decided he was ill. One night she drew down very close to him and saw the mark on his arm, and then she knew. She knew why she had come.

As swiftly as Ebis the Black's troops moved northward, the two foxes who accompanied them moved faster, impatient at the slowness of horses. They left the riders behind a mile, two miles, three, as they fled for Baylentha's shore in a frenzy to see the dragon. For already they had sighted her overhead in the moonlight, and if luck held, they might warn her of the trap.

When they topped the last hill, they plunged to a halt and stared down directly below them at Sivich and his men, all asleep in the moonlight. The trap was huge, and they could see Tebriel curled up in a corner of it; and already the dragon was storming in over the sea.

She dropped down out of the sky, directly over the trap.

"The door is propped open with a stick," said Luex. "Oh, she'll be caught!" The two foxes knew quite well about traps; they had seen many of their small, mute brothers, the red foxes, caught in them.

"She's avoiding the door. She knows about traps," said Faxel, and he watched the dragon's descent with admiration.

"She's beautiful, like snow and sea foam," breathed Luex.

"She's looking in at the prince. How can he sleep, when she is there beside him?"

"Maybe he's just lying still. Maybe he's afraid," Luex said sensibly. "He doesn't *know*. No one has told him. . . ."

Teb lay half awake, feverish and chilled, his chest hurting so, it was agony to move. When the strong, sudden wind touched his face, he rolled over, gasping with the pain—and he was staring up between the log bars at the dragon.

She blotted out the stars, hovering above him. She stared down, and her huge eyes held him. A mountain might have been swinging in the sky above him, except this mountain looked and looked, its eyes like two green pools, seeing deep inside him, seeing more than any creature should see, more than he himself knew.

At last she tore her gaze away and circled the cage, and then, as Teb's heart thudded, she dropped down to earth and stood with her shoulders pressing against the cage and her head thrusting in through the bars at him, her mouth inches from his face.

"What will she do?" whispered Luex.

"What's keeping Ebis?" Faxel grumbled. "Horses are so slow."

But though they couldn't yet hear the pounding of approaching troops, the earth had begun to tremble under their paws, so Ebis wasn't far behind.

The dragon remained very still, poised over Tebriel.

The soldiers began to wake, and the two foxes crouched lower. The camp had seemed as if dead, even the tethered horses nodding where they stood, their knees locked, quite gone in sleep standing up.

"I think that's Sivich there," said Luex, gesturing with her nose.

"How can you tell?"

"That great dark leather cape thrown over him, and the way he has the best place by the fire. But what *is* the dragon doing?"

"She still has her head in the trap," he said impatiently.

"I can see that. But why?"

"It's Sivich, all right. He sees her." They both hugged the ground as Sivich leaped up shouting.

"To arms—arm yourselves—the dragon . . . Chase it into the trap. . . . Use your spears, force it in!"

Men leaped up half dressed, grabbing swords and spears, hastily fitting arrow to bow, and soon the dragon was surrounded from behind and forced against the cage. The foxes stared and shivered as she faced her attackers, then turned away from them again almost disdainfully, and gave her attention to the boy, forcing and worrying at the great logs of his prison.

"Oh, fly away . . ." whispered Luex. "Fly away. . . ."

"She's trying to free the boy," breathed Faxel.

Bellowing, and her breath flaming, the dragon tore at the log bars. Suddenly out of the sky burst a second dragon, black as caves. He descended straight down to the female. At the same moment the pounding of hooves grew to thunder, and Ebis's troops roared into view around the hill, straight toward Sivich's army.

They rode into the midst of the soldiers, scattering

horses, charging the men who thrust and slashed at the dragon. The black dragon was battling beside her now, bellowing and throwing men against the timbers.

Then suddenly out of the maze a small figure darted, dodging beneath dragon wings and around galloping, rearing horses.

"He's free! Oh, she's freed him!" Luex yipped.

As Sivich's troops were driven back, and the black dragon nudged the female skyward, the foxes lost sight of Teb. The two dragons rose against the sky, belching flame down on the warriors; they were above the battle, covering the sky, then lifting toward the moon.

"Where is the prince?" The foxes sought that small running shape, but the battle was terrible now, as Ebis's men pounded Sivich's raiders. Had Tebriel escaped? Or had he fallen beneath pounding hooves?

"There . . ." Luex cried. "There—the prince . . . Someone has taken him up. . . . " They could see Teb then, limp and clinging in front of a rider who sped and dodged away from the battle, whipping his horse, holding the boy against him.

"It's Ebis's sergeant," said Faxel. "The white horse . . ." But six riders were converging on the fleeing soldier, their bows raised. They fired, the white horse stumbled, ran, stumbled again under a second volley, and fell, the rider spilling under its shoulder, trying to throw Teb free.

Riders and horse lay in a heap. The battle raged around them, and a rider leaped down and nudged the bodies with his toe, stood watching a moment, then mounted again and was off. The three lay unmoving.

"Are they dead?" Luex looked at Faxel, her eyes huge. They fled down the hill and onto the battlefield between rearing, plunging horses and swinging swords. They reached Teb and nuzzled his cheek with their noses.

"He's breathing," Luex panted. "But the horse— it's lying on his leg. Is it alive? Bite at it."

They bit and harried at the white gelding until, tossing in agony from its wounds and from this new torment, it heaved itself away from Teb, freeing him. But he did not move.

It was then, as they stood nosing Teb and licking his face, that suddenly the jackal broke out of a clashing melee, bloody from the fighting, dripping blood from its jaws, and was on them; neither had seen the jackal or known one was near, and they both faced it now frozen with shock before Faxel let out a staccato yipping challenge and attacked it as it bore down on them; Luex close behind screamed her fury, their sharp teeth going for its throat.

But it was a big jackal, twice their size, and maddened already from battle, and though they matched it they could not best it. When it grabbed Luex by the throat, Faxel tore at its eyes until it dropped her, then, "Run, Luex—find shelter," he yipped, and they were both dodging among fallen bodies and writhing horses as the heavy jackal winged over them. "Keep low—

under that horse. . . . It will tire before we do,"
breathed Faxel as it dropped and doubled over them.
"Keep it following, away from the boy."

Teb woke squirming with pain. His ribs were on
fire, and his leg hurt so much it sent pain all through
his body, and his vision would not come clear. He
reached out and felt a great hairy bulk. He pushed at
it and felt the inert stillness of death. He rolled away
from it, instinctively, into shelter and felt the marsh
grass bend and snap up around him as he pulled himself
through it, squirming, pulling himself in deeper across
the mud, the pain in his leg hitting him in waves as
he moved, but the sounds of battle behind him keeping
him moving. He drew in where the grass was tall and
thick, then fainted again from the pain.

The marsh lay bright green all along the coast clear
from the Bay of Fear, the eel grass and wild oats and
cord grass heavy and tall and rich with the life of crabs
and shrimps and water snails and small hatchling fishes
in among its waters. Otters hunted there sometimes,
as now did two young males out alone on a roving
spree. They sat taking a meal of oysters from a muddy
bed among the sprouting grasses when they heard the
high yipping. They had been hearing the sounds of
battle for some time, feeling the tremble of the earth
in the marsh mud.

"That's a kit fox barking," said Mikkian.

"Are you sure? All I hear is horses thudding and

humans shouting." Charkky stared toward the barrier of tall sea grass, trying to imagine what was occurring beyond it. Then the yipping of kit foxes came again. "Oh, yes—I hear it, too."

"Why would kit foxes be mixed in a battle with the dark raiders?" said Mikkian.

"I don't know. But I know dragons were mixed in."

"You only think you saw dragons. Why would—"

"I saw them, I tell you. If you hadn't been stuffing your face with oysters, you'd have seen them, too. Two dragons, Mikk. I saw. . . ."

"Hah," Mikk huffed as if he didn't believe a word.

"Well, I did see them. And I heard the foxes cry just now, as well as you did, and *I* am going to find out what's happening." And off went Charkky, humping through the tall, waving grass.

Mikkian sighed and slid up out of the mud, to follow. "We'll make better time by water," he said, nipping at Charkky's fat tail.

Charkky didn't answer, but he swerved and doubled back and headed for the surf, so the grass thrashed above him.

They dove into the breakers and were quickly beyond them, to head west, following Baylentha's shore, swimming mostly underwater, and so with no more arguing, for the moment. They reached the scene of battle and slid in under the waves, then stuck their noses out very close to shore, to hear the scream of a dying horse and smell the stench of blood. They didn't see the foxes, only the teeming battle, and they heard a groan. Then Mikk caught the scent of the foxes, and they followed it into the marsh grass, near a dead white gelding.

"The foxes were here," said Mikk. "Two of them, and—"

"I can smell them!" said Charkky. "There!" he cried, and leaped forward to part the thick grass.

Before them lay a still, bloodied human form.

"It's no bigger than we are," Mikk said, sniffing at Teb's face. "It's just a child—a boy child."

"Is it alive?"

They put their noses to Teb's nose and could feel his breath. Teb groaned again.

It took the two otters some time to decide what to do. Because the boy was small, he appealed to them more than an adult; they would likely have left an adult human to die. This boy was no older than they, and he was in need.

"They'll trample him," Mikk growled as a skirmish of fighting closed in on them. "Drag him farther into the marsh."

They did. "What now?" Charkky said. "We can't leave him. We'll have to take him home. But how? He's too sick ever to swim."

"Human boys can't swim much anyway. We—we'll have to make a raft."

"Like a fish raft for the winter catch," said Charkky.

"Exactly."

Soon Charkky was chewing off great hanks of cord grass and braiding them into twine, while Mikk searched for driftwood logs along the shore, where they had dragged Tebriel. The battle moved off to the north, away from them, so the otters worked with less frenzy. They dragged three good logs together and laced them tight, then pulled the raft into the surf, dragging Teb on board before it was quite floating, then pulling the whole heavy mass out into the waves. The journey that followed nearly killed Teb, for he almost drowned in the cold seas that lapped over him, choking him again and again. The otters had to stop pulling and pushing the raft each time and hold his head up until he could breathe. The salt water started his wounds bleeding harder, and stung fiercely.

"The blood will attract sharks and killer fish," said Mikk. "Maybe we should have left him."

"He'd have died," said Charkky.

"If you have any ideas about how to explain bringing a human home to the island, I'd like to hear them."

"It was your idea, too."

"I'm having second thoughts, is all."

"We'll just have to tell Thakkur the truth," Charkky said, shaking spray from his whiskers. "There's nothing else one can do, with Thakkur."

When Teb woke again, confused and frightened to find himself adrift in the sea, Charkky dove for sea urchins and opened them for him. Then, seeing the boy was too sick to eat properly, he shelled the urchins and chewed them, then spat them into Teb's mouth. Teb was too weak to resist, and the rich protein seemed to give him strength.

By late afternoon they had worked their way around the coast past the Bay of Fear, and past Cape Bay, into the deep shelter of the Bay of Ottra, and to the wetlands that marked the Rushmarsh Colony. The two otters had cousins and all manner of relatives here. They were surrounded at once by a crowd of inquisitive otters chittering and staring and shouting questions, otters so thick in the water around the raft that Teb could have walked to shore on their heads.

"What is it?" shouted a curious young otter, splashing up to the raft.

"It's a human," Mikk said shortly, scowling at him.

"What are you going to do with it?"

"It's not an *it*. It's a *he*. He's hurt; we're taking him home to Nightpool."

An old otter, heavily whiskered and portly, came to float on his back near the raft, ogling Teb. "They won't let you keep him. The council won't allow such a thing."

"That's silly," said Mikk. "Why wouldn't they? Mitta can doctor him, she—"

"It's no good having a human at Nightpool. Having a human know its secrets. You should know better, young Mikk."

"He's only young, like us. He wouldn't—"

"So much the more reason. Ekkthurian will never allow it."

"Ekkthurian is only one of the council, and he is not the leader," Mikkian said. "Thakkur won't turn him away." But he wondered if he was right. He wondered what Thakkur would say.

And he wondered if he dared to suggest they spend the night in Rushmarsh. They could not make it home before dark, and he didn't much like the thought of traveling with the smell of blood from the boy's leg all around them, in waters where sharks were known to swim. He saw the Rushmarsh leader swimming out toward them, his pale tan head clearly visible among the crowds of darker, teeming otters.

"Feskken will let him spend the night here," Mikk said boldly.

"He never will," said the portly otter. "Never."

8

The dragons' mating dance grew frenzied; they raced between tall white clouds, banked and leaped through Tirror's winds, while below them the seas spun away, scattered with strings of small island continents like emerald beads upon the indigo water. The winds twisted and changed direction, driven by the dragons themselves, caught in raging and time-honored passion.

At first, Dawncloud wanted to turn back to Tebriel, but her breeding cycle was very close. It was the only time the eggs could be made fertile, and this breeding was so important, for she and the male might be the last singing dragons in all of Tirror. She knew she had loosed Tebriel—she had seen him run. She began to sense at last, with the feel of rightness that sometimes came to her, that the boy was safe, that there was someone to keep him now, tenderly feed and warm him. Such a little while more, in the dragon's time sense, that the child need be tended and watched over.

The male bellowed to shake the peaks and breathed lightning and flame into the sky, so the winds grew searing hot and beat around the twining two with gale force. The male was old; this would be his last breeding. He was heavier and much larger than she, and of rougher build, but he was as graceful as a male can be in the mating dance. When Dawncloud's inner clock was sure, she rose directly into the sunset and he followed her, and they danced the final rituals, then bred high above Tirror in the orange-stained sky.

The old male died soon after breeding. The female mourned him briefly, then left him on the stony ridge. She moved high above clouds, south toward Lair Island, toward the peak on which she herself had been hatched, toward that jutting tangle of bare mountains that rises between Dubla and Fendreth-Teching. She sensed other creatures there, but they would soon be gone, for she would allow no threat to her eggs.

In Rushmarsh the crowd of otters exclaimed over Teb. Their leader, Feskken of the pale tan coat and dark muzzle, escorted the raft to shore, scowling at the few who complained and sending them on other business. "The boy will die without rest. He needs food and quiet until morning."

Charkky and Mikk looked at Feskken gratefully and pushed the raft in among the grasses of Rushmarsh, where they would be safe for the night. There they fed Teb again with chewed seafood and told their tale to Feskken and the gathering of otters in the great meeting holt in the center of Rushmarsh, a holt woven of the living green grasses of the marsh and so quite invisible from any distance, as were all the holts in Rushmarsh. Feskken sent two otters to pack Teb's wounds with damp moss and to feed him horserush tea to ease the pain. Teb hardly knew he ate or drank, and kept falling in and out of consciousness. The horserush tea made him sleep, and he knew nothing more until he woke the next morning on the raft again when the first wave hit him. He was sweating with pain again and shivering, and the otters were afraid for him. They gave him more of the tea, carefully stored in a clamshell, and again the pain eased, and Teb lay watching the sea roll and heave, and drowsing.

"Mitta will help him," Charkky said. "She'll know what to do." He splashed more cold salty water over the seaweed that packed Teb's leg and touched the boy's cheek with a hesitant paw. Teb only blinked at him. "I wish he could tell us his name," said Charkky. But Teb couldn't, he couldn't dredge any name up out of the darkness.

"He's weary with pain," Mikk said. "He's half gone in shock and sickness."

The journey took half the day, the two otters pushing and pulling the raft, a slow cumbersome way to travel for those who could flip through the sea like hawking swallows, weightless and free. By the time they sighted Nightpool, both were weary indeed of the slow, willful raft that bucked and halted at every wave. Teb had thrown up twice and was so white they were sure he would die.

"We shouldn't have brought him," said Mikk. "We should have left him on the battlefield."

"You know you couldn't have."

"What *is* Thakkur going to say?"

"What is Ekkthurian going to say is more the question."

"Who cares what Ekkthurian says. He's nothing but a troublemaker."

"Well, whatever anyone says, it'll come soon enough. Look, they're gathered on the cliff, and there's Thakkur."

The dragon took one meal after the breeding, dropping down onto a mountain pasture to snatch up sheep and goats. She ate only the aged and crippled, hunting the domestic mammals as the wolf hunts, for food only, and selectively. She had seen other dragons below her as she traveled, common dragons lairing in the mountains over which she flew, but there were none like herself. None frightened her, though if they came for her eggs, she would kill them.

At midmorning she took possession of the entire

tangle of peaks that made up the Lair, driving out two common dragons, several king lizards, and a black python, and eating their eggs and newborn so they would not return to their nests. Then she began to uproot trees from the countryside below and, on the highest peak of the Lair, to weave her nest from the trunks, curving the smaller branches and twigs inward to make a soft bed. She sensed the five young within her with a terrible joy of love and possession.

When she was ready to lay, she killed two angora goats and three sheep, and laid them around the nest in a circle, then ripped their bellies open. These would receive her five eggs, to warm and nurture them. When all was ready, she crouched, bellowed again to shake the sky, and began to lay.

Teb's first view of Nightpool was a towering black rock jutting up out of the pounding sea. Then of a crowd of otters silhouetted along the high cliff looking down at him; then, like birds swooping, they dove into the sea and came up bobbing all around him, chattering and sending the raft rocking. Pretty soon he was being carried up the steep cliff, biting his lip against the pain of movement. It was all like a disjointed dream—some parts fuzzy, or filled only with physical pain, then a scene coming suddenly clear. Then he was in a cave, lying on a low stone shelf, and otters stood looking down at him. One, a plump female, began to examine his leg, feeling the broken bones with fingers so gentle they were like the touch of a moth. She felt Teb's fevered face, then began barking directions in a sharp, keening voice that sent young otters flying out the door. "I want wood for splints. Get straight driftwood. I want horserush, crush it well and make the tea with it, stir it and stir it until it is all brown. I want moss dampened in the sea, and braided eelgrass for binding the splints. And I want fresh clay in the biggest clamshell, well moistened."

When she had sent the young otters away, she sat with her paw on Teb's forehead, studying his face, her big dark eyes very gentle. He could hear voices outside the cave, and some of them were angry. Arguments flew in and out of his consciousness as he dozed and woke.

Once he felt his head lifted, and then he tasted the familiar horserush brew. And then later he felt a tug at his clothes and saw that the female otter was cutting away his trousers with a sharp clamshell. His boots were already gone. She undid his tunic, lifted him again, and slid it off, then covered him with a thick moss blanket. The chain was gone from his leg. It had been on his left leg. It was his right leg that was so filled with pain. He thought he remembered something like flame searing off the chain, but nothing would come clear. There were voices somewhere nearby, still arguing, but there was no one in the cave save the small, pudgy female. He could hear the argument clearly.

"The boy can't be kept here; such a thing is impossible."

"Of course we'll keep him. He needs help."

"He won't even tell us his name. I call that suspicious."

"He *can't* tell us his name. Can't you see how sick he is?"

"It's far too dangerous to have a human here. It's never been done," said the querulous voice. Teb tried to shut the voices out. The pain was coming back, and he felt sick.

"Hah! Thakkur can't let him stay. The council will vote him down." And then the voices grew silent suddenly.

Teb saw a white otter enter the cave, rearing tall, his coat like snow against the dark stone wall. He stood looking down at Teb, searching his face with great dark eyes.

"I am Thakkur," he said quietly. Then, "Come, Mitta, let's look at the leg." He pulled the moss cover back, then scowled, touching Teb's leg delicately. "It's twice the size of the other leg and purple as sea urchins. Can we heal it?"

"We will try."

"And what are those scars on his ankles? Old scars— as if chains had been wrapped around them."

"Slaves are chained," she said. She covered Teb to the waist with the moss blanket. "The ribs are hurt,

106

too. And there are old, healed scars on his back. As from lashings with a whip."

Thakkur lifted Teb's shoulders gently, to look. The smell of him, as of all the otters, was a fishy breath. He laid Teb down again, and his dark eyes were expanding pools into which Teb in his half consciousness seemed to be falling.

"Can you tell us your name, child? Who are you?"

But Teb couldn't dredge it up. He shook his head feebly. The pain was too great to think, the throbbing in his leg and ribs like a drum beating, sucking him down. Mitta gave him more tea, and soon again he was dropping away into darkness, in and out of consciousness.

Then he woke a little more, for they were doing something to his leg. He lay watching them, the white otter and the smaller, rounder brown Mitta. He studied her squarish, furred face and her round dark eyes, which looked at him so gently, and her spiky, drooping whiskers. She hadn't any chin, and when she spoke, her dark nose twitched and her whiskers trembled.

"We must set the leg, Thakkur and I. We will do it as gently as we can. But there will be pain again when we pull and the bones pop into place. It cannot be helped."

He felt their paws on his leg, felt them grip and knew a surge of fear at new pain. Their paws touched his leg, investigating, searching, as he lay trying to put down the fear.

"Is the splint ready?" said the white otter.

"Yes, here. And the clay."

"All right, then. Steady now, boy. It won't take long."

And then the pain struck him so his whole body was afire and tears spurting from his eyes, and he heard a crunching of bone. Then it was over.

He felt himself covered again, felt the gentle paws, felt at last the sweet coolness as the wet clay pack was worked around his splinted leg. Then, exhausted, he slept, only vaguely aware of Mitta laying her head on his chest to listen, and then the two otters sitting nearby, talking softly.

"I'm afraid for him," Mitta said. "The clay will help soak infection from the leg, but it's more than that."

"The ribs are broken, too. We will bind them," Thakkur said.

"But look how old the cuts on his arm are. He has had a long time of being hurt, perhaps being cold and without proper food. There is a sickness there in his chest, as a creature will get when it is harried and cold and without rest."

"We can only do our best for him."

"We must get food down him. Charkky and Mikk were right to chew shellfish for him, and I will do the same."

"We can all do that, if needed. I will choose half a

dozen to help tend him, so you can return to your cubs when you wish. We can only do our best," he repeated. "And make a prayer at meeting."

"And keep Ekkthurian away from him." She raised her eyes to Thakkur. "I'm glad he is in your cave, where he will know added protection. Who is this boy? Mikk said there was a terrible battle where they found him. The dark ones, I suppose, raging and making trouble. I do wish humans could be content with the land, and with the riches we all have."

"Some humans can," said Thakkur shortly. "It's the dark ones—Quazelzeg and his kind."

"If they keep on, nothing will be safe. Nothing will be left."

Thakkur nodded. "Not even Nightpool." He patted Mitta's forepaw. "The boy will tell us more when he is well again."

Mitta looked at him doubtfully.

"He will get well, Mitta. He must. I feel it is important—that the boy is important somehow." Thakkur turned and left his cave, and Mitta settled down on a stone bench near Teb and took up her weaving again. Her paws were never idle, those busy otter paws mending and weaving and shucking shellfish, cleaning and grooming herself, changing Teb's bandages and gently feeding him.

And so began a strange, disjointed, dreamlike time for Teb, when he would wake and see daylight outside the cave, or darkness and stars, sometimes a moon, but with no idea of passing days. He was vaguely aware sometimes of being waked and his head held up, and food spooned into his mouth on a shell, of being told to swallow though he felt too tired to swallow. Aware of things done to his leg, of covers pulled over him or removed. Aware of the furred paws tending him and of the softness of otter voices, of their soft "Hah" of greeting. Strangely aware sometimes of dreams that tangled into senselessness when he tried to remember them.

Often he woke moaning with terror and visions of men with knives bending over him, and then Mitta would come and hold him like her own child and nuzzle his neck until he felt comforted.

But the terror of not knowing who he was, of not even knowing his name, could not be comforted.

9

Summer grew hot, but the sea wind helped to calm Teb's fever. The otters bathed him with cool water and fed him pulverized shellfish and roots and strange fish juices. He drifted in and out of dreams and fragmented scenes and made little sense of anything until one morning, late into the fall of the year, with the sea running warm and green and gulls screaming out over the waves, he woke at last with a clear, eager curiosity and stared around the cave where he lay, and frowned at the white otter who stood tall, looking down at him.

He tried to remember where he was, and why he was here. He tried to put together the dreams of fighting and of dragons, with the otters coming and going and the constant pounding of the sea, the pounding that filled his ears now as he gazed at a patch of sunlight across the white otter's shoulder, and then at the smaller, dark, round otter who moved beside him carrying a clamshell.

"Mitta," Teb said, "Mitta."

They helped him to sit up and placed the clamshell in his lap. He felt starved, but he stared down at the mess of raw shellfish, then looked back at them helplessly. "It's raw. It's—"

"You have been eating raw fish all summer," said the white otter. "I am Thakkur. You are in the otter colony of Nightpool."

Teb stared at Thakkur and back at the food, and almost retched. "If you could make a fire, maybe I could cook it," he said helplessly.

Mitta frowned at him. He felt tender toward her, knew she had tended him, only now she looked more angry than gentle. "We do not have fire at Nightpool. This is good food. You have been eating it all along. You need the strength it will give you." She stood glaring at Teb until he managed to down a piece of the stuff, and found it was not so bad. He ate another—an oyster, he guessed—and soon grinned up at them and finished the lot. And then he felt sleepy again, his eyes so heavy, and he dropped off, watching Mitta tuck the moss cover around him.

He woke much later in a patch of sunlight that shone down from a high opening at the back of the cave. He was alone. It was warm. He stared out through the door at the sea and felt the salt wind in his face. He looked down at the clay cast that held his leg and peered under the rumpled moss blanket to find himself naked. There were scars on his arms and thigh and chest where old wounds had healed, a scar on his arm that he stared at, frowning. It ran through a little brown mark that puzzled him, though he did not know why. He pulled the cover back over himself, and looked around at the cave, at its dark stone walls curving up to the dome overhead. Seats were carved into the walls, and shelves at different levels, and ledges for sleeping, like the one on which he lay.

The higher shelves held objects from the sea, shells of different shapes and colors, and corals. There were some bones, too, and a whitened human skull. And, in one large niche all alone, the immense jawbone of some creature with viciously sharp teeth. Teb thought it must be a shark.

When the white otter returned he sat near Teb and smiled a whiskery grin that made Teb want to laugh. Yet there was a great, calm dignity about the white otter, too.

"Thakkur," Teb said. "I remember. I guess you saved my life. I guess I don't remember much about coming here. How did I get here? How long have I been lying here?"

Thakkur's whiskers twitched. "It has been all summer, and we are now into the fall; the shad are running. You had a very high fever for a long time. You slept a good deal. I expect everything is muddled in your mind. But can you tell me your name? Can you tell me what happened to you?"

Teb tried, and when his name would not come to him, a surge of panic swept over him. He could not remember how he had gotten here, or how he had gotten hurt. He knew his leg had been broken; he could remember the otters setting it, could still remember tears springing at the sudden violent pain. But he could not remember anything before the disjointed scenes here in this cave and some confused, dark dreams that would not come clear.

"It will come," said the white otter at last. "It will come when you are stronger. Meanwhile," he said, laying a paw on Teb's arm, "you are safe here. And welcome."

But he was not welcome by everyone, Teb knew that. And he would know it more certainly soon enough.

It was some time after the white otter left that Mitta came to sit with Teb again, her paws busy now weaving grasses into a thin cord, and he remembered her sitting quietly beside him many times when he woke, and always her paws were busy working at something, or playing with the necklace of stones she wore. He saw, when he began to have visitors, that all the otters except Thakkur wore such stones.

The visitors came two and three at a time to look at him and touch him with shy, thrusting paws, rearing and grinning with whiskered smiles and fishy breath, saying, "Hah, human boy," and "Hah, you are better, human boy." They would come dripping from the sea, their thick fur all spiky from being wet, and they would come in dry and sleek and groomed, silken and beautiful. But always their paws were busy as they visited with him, playing with the worry stones usually, as if an otter's paws had not the ability to be still. Mitta sent one small cub out because it made too much fuss by jumping up onto Teb's sleeping shelf to investigate his cast with busy fingers. "Get out into the day and play with your worry stones, and leave the poor boy alone."

Otters touched his cheek with cold, damp paws. Young otters nuzzled up to him and brought him limp wildflowers, and in between visitors Teb lay looking at Thakkur's strange collection of relics from the sea. When Charkky and Mikk came to sit with him, Charkky lifted down the treasures one at a time for him to examine. There were, besides the shells and bones, some rusted tools and odd bits of metal, a hinge, a spike, gold coins and pearls, and a box made of sea-darkened maple and carved with words across its top. He fingered the carved letters but could not make meaning of them.

"I thought all humans could read," Charkky said.

"I don't know," Teb said, confused. "Only that I can't read this." He felt so empty, not to know anything about himself, not to know his name or how he had gotten to the marsh where Charkky and Mikk had found him. They told him about the battle, and about the making of the raft and their journey home, but he could not remember anything before that time. He had no idea what the battle was about, though all the otters agreed it had to do with the dark forces, and with a leader called Quazelzeg. He had no idea what he had been doing in that battle.

Strangely, he felt most at ease within himself in the evenings when he was alone in the cave with Thakkur, for the old white otter did not ask difficult questions, but instead told him the tales of the Ottra nation, fables of the sea and of magic creatures, stories that stirred some strange longing in him; as if he had heard such tales before, as if he valued them. Somehow such tales seemed a part of himself, though he had no notion how. Tales of the diving whales that would come to the surface with the sucker marks of giant squid on their black hides from deep-sea battles, tales of seabirds that could travel the entire length of the great sea without ever landing, and of the sea bat that swam deep down on wings as wide as the length of twenty otters. Tales of ghost lights deep in the sea made by the souls of drowned fishermen. Tales of drowned cities that once had stood on solid land; though it was not until much later that Thakkur explained how such a thing could be. Tales of the ghosts that were said to haunt such cities. And tales of the three-headed black hydrus that Thakkur said was so very different from the smaller land hydrus, fiercer, and foreign to this world, having entered Tirror from some other world. Though again, it was not until a later time that Thakkur would tell him how that entry was accomplished, or how deep was the sea hydrus's evil.

When Teb began to feel stronger, he grew restless, hobbling around the cave, but the clay cast was fragile, and Mitta wouldn't allow him to go very far out along the ledge. The cast was hot and itchy, too, and he longed to pull it off. Mitta said, "Not yet. I don't know how long it will take to heal; I only know about otters' legs. And yours was so very hurt. A few more weeks, and we will cut it off." But he dreamed of being free of it, and of leaping into the cool sea, free and whole, to dive and float as the otters did, to roll and play their complicated sea games with them. Though Teb had no idea whether he *could* swim. He could not remember swimming.

He moved his sleeping place to a shelf beside the door, opposite Thakkur's, where he could look directly down at the pounding waves and feel the sea spray on his face. And in the daytime he watched the otters fishing in the bright, rolling sea, their long sinuous bodies turning underwater, and he imagined how cool and silky the water must feel.

Then one morning early, Charkky and Mikk appeared at the cave door with a long, forked branch.

"It's a crutch," Charkky said, and hobbled a few

steps to demonstrate. "We padded it with moss. See?"

Teb tried it, and it worked just fine. He hobbled around the cave, grinning.

"And Mitta says you are to come and live in her cave awhile," said Mikk. "You are growing too restless. You can wander more on the inside of the island."

He walked to Mitta's cave on the new crutch, over the rocky rim of the island, flanked by Charkky and Mikk. They paused on the high rim, whipped by the sea wind, and Teb stared down at the inner island with surprise. "It's hollow." A bright green valley lay far down in the cupped center of Nightpool, rich with meadow, and with a little lake and a brilliant green marsh and, at the far side of the valley just below the rising black cliff, a long body of water that was an inner sea, moving and churning like the great sea. He could see a black tunnel at the south end through which the sea was flowing in. The inner cliffs, around the meadow, were lined with dwelling caves. "It's all hidden, the whole valley. No one would ever know."

Charkky and Mikk grinned at his appreciation.

Below them in the little lake, a dozen otter cubs were playing catch with a shell, tossing it far out, and diving and squealing. At Mitta's cave, her own three cubs overwhelmed Teb with chittering and hugging, and the smallest climbed right up his good leg, to cling to his neck, tickling his throat with her whiskers.

So it was that Teb moved into Mitta's cave, with a sleeping shelf by the door, where he could come and go as he liked. From here, with the help of the crutch, he could make his way down to the little valley and wander among the tall bright grasses beside the marsh, watching the water birds fly up and small snakes slip away from him, watching the otters at food gathering.

He missed Thakkur, though, and the long evenings of storytelling. He went back often, but it was not quite the same as listening to Thakkur's tales curled up under the cover, ready for sleep. And there was no strong pounding of the sea in Mitta's cave, only a faint echo accompanying the sleepy whimpers of the cubs. Teb began to put himself to sleep by trying out different stories about himself. Was he a fisherman's son? A blacksmith's helper? Where had the scars come from? No story he could imagine seemed to stir a memory, even that of a slave, though it would explain the scars. And then one morning, Mitta found the note.

She had laid his bloody tunic and ripped trousers away at the back of her cave and given him a moss wrap to wear. But one morning early the three tumbling cubs found the clothes and pulled them out and began a rough game with them until Mitta returned and snatched them away. As she straightened them, her busy paws found a piece of paper deep in the tunic pocket.

It was wrinkled and torn, and had been wet, so the writing was blurred. He stared at it and knew—he knew—but then it was gone, the knowledge gone. He tried to make out the words.

After a long time, Mitta said, "What does it tell you?"

"I can't read it," he said, puzzling. "I can see the letters plainly under the blur. But I don't know what they say." He frowned. "I can't read, Mitta. I don't know how to read." He felt strange and empty. Surely he had known how to read; he was not a baby, but half grown.

"Is it such a bad thing not to know how to read?" Mitta said. "Otters don't know how."

"I think it's a bad thing for humans." He stared at the paper, perplexed. But it was not until two days later, when he had picked it up for the hundredth time to try to puzzle it out, that he suddenly saw one word in a new way and could read it.

"Tebriel!" he shouted, startling the tumbling cubs. "Tebriel! My name is Tebriel."

The three cubs crowded around him. "Tebriel! Tebriel! Let us see!"

"Right here," he said, pointing. "Plain as your whiskers, it says 'Tebriel.' "

They glided up onto his knees and stared at the crumpled paper, but it was only blurred squiggles to their eyes.

"If you can read your name," said Mitta, "can you read the rest?"

"No," he said, frowning at the faded paper.

"Is the paper so very important?"

120

"It might tell me who I am."

"But you know who," cried the cubs. "You are Tebriel. Teb, Teb, Tebriel," they chattered.

"I don't know who, though. I don't know who Tebriel is."

"Perhaps Thakkur can conjure a vision that will tell you," said Mitta. "In the sacred shell, in the great hall. Your name will help him, something to bring the vision."

"He can do it," cried the bigger male cub.

"He can do it at the meeting to decide . . ." began the female, then looked distressed.

"Meeting to decide what?" said Teb.

Mitta sighed. "You will have to know soon enough." The cubs were silent now.

"To decide about you," Mitta said. "To decide whether you can stay at Nightpool. It will be voted on. Some . . . some of the clan want to send you away."

"Oh," Teb said. "I see. Well, I am well now; my leg is all but mended. I can go away now."

"And where would you go, when you don't know who you are? There are the scars of a whip on your back, Tebriel. And the marks of a chain on your ankle. Do you think you can wander across Tirror in any safety when you don't know whom to trust, and who might again make you a prisoner?"

"Then I must wait for the vision to tell me."

"If Thakkur can bring a vision. It is not always so.

Sometimes it takes much more than the germ of a word to bring knowledge through the sacred shell." Mitta pulled a squirming cub to her and fondled his ears. "Thakkur's visions are not such an easy magic as young cubs would like to believe."

1O

Across the vast floor of the meeting cave, otters drew close to one another in untidy groups, a mass of dark velvet with gleaming dark eyes flashing looks at one another. On the stone dais at the back, Thakkur, white against the dark coats of the twelve council members, stood at prayer.

The walls of the cave were set with pieces of shells of all kinds, in every color a shell can be, to make pictures, the pictures of animals, so that Teb was caught in a memory that stirred him terribly. What was this feeling? What was he trying to remember? He sat on a stone bench against the wall of the cave, between Charkky and Mikk, staring around at the animal pictures caught in a shaft of sunlight, and could almost see other pictures, another place very like this; yet when he tried to bring his thoughts clear, that other place vanished.

He studied these pictures, frowning. They showed otters. And foxes. Wolves and great cats and one old badger. They showed three unicorns. They showed a whole cloud of owls flying. And on the wall behind the dais was the picture that stirred him most. There, caught in flight, was an immense dragon, her wings spread halfway round the walls as she twisted in flight, gleaming. She struck him dumb with wonder, with recognition, with awe and yearning and confusion.

He could not understand his emotions, and the more he tried the more confused he got, until his mind churned into a muddle and he gave it up, and attended instead to Thakkur's prayers.

They were gentle prayers of joy, and of thanksgiving for the good run of fishes, the good and plentiful yields of oysters and clams and periwinkles, and all the crops the otters harvested. And then a prayer of thanksgiving, too, for Teb himself, that he had healed and was well again. And then Thakkur turned to face the giant clamshell that stood upright on a stone pedestal at the center back of the dais. The cave became hushed as the white otter raised his paws, then stood motionless, his back very straight. He spoke so softly Teb could not make out the words, but soon the concave face of the shell began to shine with a smoky light. Vague shadows moved across it. Thakkur spoke Teb's name three times, then waited. No image came clear, and again he spoke. "Tebriel. Tebriel."

No image formed, and at long last the shadows across the shell vanished. Thakkur turned to face the gathered otters, and a sigh of disappointment filled the cave.

"I can bring nothing clear. I can bring no image to show us who you are, Tebriel."

"Then," spoke up Ekkthurian sharply, "we will discuss what to do with the boy."

Beside Teb, Charkky sat up straighter, his whiskers twitching with anger. "The devil take Ekkthurian," he said softly. "The sharks take him!"

Mikkian sat very still, one paw lifted to his whiskers in a stiff, arrested gesture. Then he turned to look at Teb, his whiskers bristling and his round dark eyes flashing, and a little growl deep in his throat. "Don't pay any attention to what he's going to say. Old Ekkthurian's nothing but a grouch."

But the sense of peace and unity that the prayers had brought, and that Thakkur's attempt at vision had brought, dissolved as Ekkthurian rose from his place in the council ring, his voice harsh and hissing.

"The boy is healed. His fever is cured. His limb mended. I saw him walk here to the meeting cave by himself, on the sapling crutch. I say it is time he move on. Nightpool is not meant for humans."

"What reasons do you have for hurrying our guest away?" asked Thakkur.

"We do not receive guests at Nightpool, except others of the clan. We never have. Only the otters of Rushmarsh are welcome."

"Has that been put to a vote?" inquired Thakkur.

"No vote is needed. That is our custom."

"It was not the custom when Nightpool was a sanctuary. When it stood along the old road before the causeway collapsed, no wanderer was turned away, human or animal. Who changed our customs?"

"Those days are gone. This is not that time; that time is long past. Humans traveling the land now cannot be trusted."

"Do you question the boy's honesty?"

"There is no commerce anymore between us who speak with honest tongue and the human horde. They have proven themselves untrustworthy."

"Not all humans are of a kind," said Thakkur. "Any more, Ekkthurian, than are any race."

"There is no perfidy or dishonesty among our race."

"That," said Thakkur, "is a matter of opinion. Now I put the matter to vote. Know you all that the boy has, at this time, no other safe sanctuary save Nightpool. He does not know who he is or where he belongs. He has been kept as slave by someone, for there are the marks of irons on his ankles and the scars of a whip on his back." Thakkur seemed very tall, there on the dais. "If we turn away one innocent human boy who has been so mistreated, know you that all of us will suffer soon enough at the hands of his abusers."

"How do you know such a thing?" barked Ekkthurian. "Is that a prophecy?"

"It is a prophecy," Thakkur said shortly. He stood looking at the council members coolly, his white body gleaming in the morning light. Then he looked down to the gathered otters. "The clan will vote, not the council."

"No!" cried Ekkthurian. "The council—"

"Yes," Thakkur said. "This is a matter for all to decide and takes no special knowledge of the fishing waters, which is the council's purpose." Thakkur looked down over the brown velvet mass of otters. "Those who would send the boy away, please stand."

Perhaps a dozen otters stood up, some of them sheepishly. One young otter looked around him and sat down again.

"Now those who would give him sanctuary."

The velvet floor seethed, as all over the cave otters rose up. Then all heads turned to look at Teb. And when the council left the dais, a crowd of otters gathered around him, standing tall to touch and stroke him. Mikk and Charkky hugged him so hard, they nearly toppled him and had to pick up his fallen crutch. Then Mitta was there—hugging, too, and giving him a wet lick on the ear.

"And when you grow tired of my crowded cave, Tebriel, and the ruckus of the cubs, Thakkur has said you may have a cave of your own."

So it was that, when at last he put his crutch aside

and could walk the cliffs of Nightpool with only a small clay cast, Teb chose his own cave and moved into it. Though the moving was simple enough: his moss bed cover, his old bloodied tunic and trousers and boots, the note he had carried, and a clamshell for eating. He chose a cave down island from Thakkur's, jutting high above the pounding waves and with salt spray coming in and the rising sun to wake him. It had seven shelves for his possessions and a single sleeping shelf. A cave for a bachelor otter, such as Mikk and Charkky shared, and at once it was home to him and seemed wonderful.

The year was coming on toward winter now, and turning cold, and Mitta found him a second moss blanket, for, as she pointed out, he had no fur to warm him. He cut and tied a breechcloth from his old, torn trousers and donned the tunic again. And as the winds turned chill, Mitta began to weave him a gull-feather blanket.

She sent all the young otters along the cliffs gathering feathers and moss, and Teb made a loom for her by tying four driftwood poles into a square and lacing it with grass rope, as she directed. The weaving began well, thick and soft, and Teb took Mitta's place gathering oysters and clams so she could work on it.

He gathered cattail root and water herbs, too, from the freshwater lake, but he was growing very tired of raw food and longed for roast mutton and fresh-baked bread. He longed to be swimming, too, for the late fall turned hot suddenly, and even the small cast itched and made him hot all over. Though he did not know whether he *could* swim, and he thought it so strange that he could remember vividly roast mutton and good things to eat, yet could remember nothing of real importance about himself, who he was or where he belonged. He watched the otters fishing in the sea and playing, flying through the clear water, darting and twisting. He watched them floating, napping in the sea anchored in the rocking beds of kelp, watched the mothers carrying their cubs on their backs or rocking them on their stomachs, watched Mikk and Charkky's scouting band of young otters go out to track the fish migrations, and he felt left out and alone.

There were three little bays at the north end of the island, and here in these sheltered places the seaweed was thick, and the periwinkles and little mud crabs grew. One bay had a shingle beach that he explored and tide pools to poke into. He watched the bright, small sea creatures that lived there, ruffled snails and anemones that looked like flowers, and he walked the rocky oyster beds that spread north from the island's tip, exposed at low tide, and gathered the oysters, prying them up with a thick fragment of shell. But he was restless and longed to be out in the sea. He explored the island's wave-tossed beaches with Charkky and Mikk, and they showed him, from the far north end of the oyster beds, a deep undersea trench that ran out from the mainland, dropping down across the undersea shelf toward the deeps. The otters preferred to stay in the shallower waters above the wide shelf, where the fish were plentiful and the larger creatures of the sea—the great eels and the giant squid and huge sharks—did not usually come. Teb could see the mark of the undersea trench, like a drowned river, on the land, too, where the high cliff broke into a ravine and spilled out a little stream. When the tide was in, the seaweed and mud flat were disturbed, and the little creatures that lived there moved about, drawing great flocks of gulls to dive and feed. And the highest tides splashed their waves into the northernmost caves of Nightpool, giving the occupants wet floors, which the otters seemed to find delightful.

He watched the otters humping through the sea in smooth shallow dives, then floating facedown so they could see the fish beneath the water. He watched them dive deep, to come up below a fish where it could not see them, to grab it from below, then surface. They would lie on their backs eating the squirming creatures with relish.

A larger bay opened toward the south end of the island, with a jutting arm of land to protect it, and it made a fine place to drive big schools of fish in toward land, the otters working together as men would herd horses, driving the fish nearly onto the shore, then grabbing as many as they could hold and stuffing them into large string bags. Teb was watching such a drive one morning when he turned to see Ekkthurian atop a jutting rock, watching him. He smiled at the thin, dark otter and tried to talk to him, but Ekkthurian scowled and turned away, and later Teb saw him with his two companions, talking angrily to Thakkur, just beside the great cave.

He came on them suddenly and heard Ekkthurian saying, "He is leading the young otters in unnatural ways, Charkky and Mikk spend too much time with him, and the small cubs are beginning to look up to him and to repeat things he says, such as that cooked food tastes delicious, that a steel knife would pry up oysters better than a shell does. They are otters, not humans, and they must not forget it. The boy is not a good influence."

Teb slipped away, not wanting to hear more, and stayed off by himself for the rest of the day. But that night, as he sat at supper with Mitta and her cubs, she said, "You are sad, Tebriel."

"No, not really."

"You will remember one day who you are and where you came from," she said. "And you will have the cast off soon."

"I know."

"Meantime, though, it's hard to be patient."

"Yes." He didn't tell her what really bothered him. It is an ugly feeling to know you are not wanted, even by only a few.

"Have you tried again to read the small paper you carried?"

"Yes. It seems it ought to come right, that if I looked

at it just the right way, I could read it. But I never can."

"There is some writing in the great cave. Could that help?"

"Where?"

"On the walls among the pictures. A few marks, all together in one place, just to the left of the entry." She saw his excitement and grinned. "Go, then. Go and look."

He went slowly over the rim of the island, impatient at his clumsiness in the cast, then stood at last in the great cave, alone. It was dim now in the fading light. He approached the dais and stood looking at the sacred clamshell, remembering the only prophecy that Thakkur had been able to bring forth about him, that somehow he was linked to the fate of Tirror and so, too, to the fate of Nightpool. But how? What could such a prophecy mean? At last he turned away.

The words were all together as Mitta had said, one beneath each animal leader, fox and otter and wolf, owl and great cat. Teb studied each word and knew that the separate letters made the sounds of the animals' names. He had a vague memory of someone showing him how this could be, someone saying the sounds of the letters, but he could not dredge up who, or where that had happened.

He stayed in the cave a long time, fitting sounds to letters the way he thought they should be. There was no word for badger or unicorn, or for the dragon. He stood looking up at the dragon with a terrible yearning that left him puzzled and excited.

He returned to his cave to unfold the paper, to try again to read.

It was a long message. He sounded out some of the letters, and tried to make words, but it wasn't much help. He thought one word might be "of" and the one before it "care." He could not guess at the rest, could make no sense of the carefully penned, faded lines. He put it away again, under a round rock on the shelf, and stood idly watching a band of otters floating on their backs in the green swells, cracking sea urchins open with their worry stones and eating them, tossing the shells into the waves. And it was as he stood there that something strange began to happen in his thoughts, that a song began to form, clear and rhythmic, speaking of the sea and the otters, a song that made itself. When it was finished, he remembered every word.

A verse came about Mitta, and about Charkky and Mikk, about Thakkur, until as he sat in his cave door musing, dozens of verses were formed, painting clearly the life around him, the joy and animal wildness of Nightpool, and each verse a little song in itself to cheer and entertain him. He knew he would remember them all without effort, and he wondered how that could be, when he couldn't remember anything at all about himself.

It was the day that Mitta cut the last cast from his leg with a sharpened shell, and massaged his leg and pronounced it mended, that she said, "I think you must begin to cook your meals, Tebriel. You are not looking well, and you are eating less and less."

He stared at Mitta. Cooked food would taste wonderful. "But cook how? There's no way to make fire, Mitta. You need flint."

Mitta glanced at the tumbling cubs, then sent them out to play. When they were gone, she said quietly, "You must steal what you need to make fire."

He stared at her. "Steal it where? And what would Thakkur say?"

"Thakkur agrees with me. You are too thin and pale. Maybe raw food does not agree with you." She touched Teb's hand with a gentle paw. "Charkky and Mikk will go with you; they will like another ramble before winter. You will take the raft. You can steal what you need from the place of battle where they found you. Steal it from the dead."

Teb sat quiet for some time. Mitta turned to her weaving, working feathers in with moss. Already the blanket was a fourth finished. She said nothing until Teb said suddenly, "You think if I go there, I'll remember. Who I am, and what happened to me there."

She looked at him evenly, a wild, steady look, the kind of look a hunting otter fixes on its prey.

"Perhaps, Tebriel. Do you think it is worth trying?"

It was later that he wondered uneasily if he was afraid to go back there, afraid of remembering. But that was silly. They would go there to the coast of

Baylentha, and he would find, somewhere among the bodies, which by now must be nothing but skeletons, the small striking flint he would need to make fire, and maybe a pan to cook in, maybe a good knife dropped and forgotten. And maybe he would find himself, maybe he would meet Tebriel there and know him and know all that had happened in his life.

11

"Hah," said Charkky, "it's barely light. I'll just nip down for a flounder, on our way."

"You keep pushing the raft," said Mikk. "I'll get the flounder." He dove so suddenly he seemed to disappear, and was back in no time with a fine silvery flat fish with both its eyes on one side of its head. He bit it in half and gave the tail half to Charkky; then both otters swam along pushing the raft, each holding the great piece of fish in his mouth, chewing away. Teb watched them for a moment, then turned his attention to the gray heaving sea and the first hint of sunrise in the east where the sea met the sky. He had breakfasted on cattail root and a plant that Mitta called water lettuce, and he thought with longing of cooked food, porridge and mutton and berry pies and ham. Though he could not imagine the food in any setting, not a room, or even catch the vision of a cookfire. He knew what a flint striker would look like, though, and he hoped there would be a flint somewhere on the battleground. He had turned to watching the high cliff that marked the edge of the mainland when the raft gained speed suddenly, and four more otters popped up with dripping whiskers to stare at him as they pushed. Jukka and Hokki and Litta, three bright young females, and Kkelpin, a black scar on his shoulder showing beneath the foaming water. The raft moved so fast now Teb felt he was almost flying, and a song made itself in his head as they sped along, about the six otters and the sea and the tall black cliffs and the gulls.

"What are you grinning about?" Charkky said, poking his head up over the edge of the raft. "What are you thinking, Tebriel?"

"That I'm going as fast as king of the ocean now, and you're six fine steeds pulling me."

He got a face full of water for that, and he managed to push Charkky under, but only because Charkky let him. By midmorning the sun had burned the clouds away and the day was hot, and Teb watched the swimming otters with envy, and let his feet trail over, until he realized it made a drag on the raft.

"Come in," shouted Charkky, popping up in a distant

wave. They were taking turns now, pushing.

"Hah," said Mikk, leaping up onto the raft. "Have a swim, Tebriel."

"I don't know if I can swim. I don't remember . . ."

"We'll help you. It's simple."

"Simple for you, maybe." He was so hot and itchy, and the water was so cool. He knelt, watching the swells and wondering if he would sink. But how could he sink with six otters crowded around ready to pull him out? If he couldn't swim, though, he would look like a fool.

But then at last he could stand it no longer, and he slipped in and let the cool water take him, easy, buoying him—and he was floating.

"If you can float," said Charkky, "you can swim."

Jukka looked skeptical, her dark face close to Teb's, as if she meant to save him.

He tried wriggling as the otters did, but he went under, and when he came up they were all laughing at him.

"You're not an otter," Charkky said. "I don't think . . ."

"You've no tail for wriggling and thrusting," Jukka said, huffing at him with an otterish giggle.

"Float again," said Mikk. "Move your arms and legs; they're all you have to move when you haven't a tail."

"He doesn't even have webs between his toes," said Litta, with a small female smirk. "How can he . . . ?"

"Just do it," said Mikk, scowling at Litta.

"Don't think about it," said Kkelpin. "It will come easier if you just do what comes naturally."

Teb lay flat on his face and felt the cool salty water soothe him, and soon he was stroking out, kicking. Then he was really swimming, as if his body had known all along. He kicked and reached in a long, easy crawl in the rolling ocean, surrounded by diving, laughing otters. He glanced back to see the raft coming along, pushed by one otter, then another. He hadn't realized how much they had been slowing for him, bobbing and waiting and pacing him patiently; now he felt he was almost flying through the clear green sea.

Then at last, when the muscles of his hurt leg began to ache, he flipped back onto the raft, and again his steeds sent it speeding.

"You swim like a fish," said Charkky. "Look ahead, we're coming to the cave of the ghost."

"What is that?" Teb could see a dark cleft dividing the cliff; then when they drew closer he could see it was a cave. A clattering rose suddenly, and an immense flock of birds burst out and went sweeping away over the sea, to wheel far out, screaming.

"Cormorants," shouted Mikk.

"Is that the ghost?"

This made Charkky and Hokki laugh and dive.

"You won't see the ghost," Mikk said. "No one does; he lives on the white cliffs in the cave." They were opposite the opening now, and Teb could see that the cave was huge. A damp, cold breath blew out of it, smelling of bird droppings, and the jagged stone inside was covered with droppings heavy and white as snow.

"It is said he comes out to make the storms of the sea," said Jukka, shaking water over Teb. "That his birds stir the wind into storm, and he himself roils the sea and makes it heave and churn."

The birds returned, wheeling over them, and when the raft was past the cave, the flock swept back in and vanished. And suddenly a song filled Teb's mind with words crying in his head, and he sat wondering at it and examining it as the tall cliffs passed, for it was not just a song about the ghost and the things he was seeing, but stretched far back in time, a song alive with wrecked ships and drowned cities and things he had never known.

Or, things he *thought* he had never known—but how could he tell?

He watched Charkky dive down to retrieve oysters from the undersea caves, then lie on his back shucking and eating them. He could not see the land above the cliffs—they were far too tall—but green grass hung over where some of the cliff had crumbled out from beneath the turf. And once, just beyond the cave of the ghost, he saw horses silhouetted against the sky, and that, too, made a yearning in him, so he could almost smell their sweet scent and feel them warm and silky beneath his hands.

Why did it all stay hidden? And what was the song

that had come, so different from the others? Why did it make him lonely?

The sun was just overhead when they came to the Bay of Ottra and were surrounded at once by a mob of splashing, diving, huffing otters. He remembered the sea alive with them when he had come this way before, shaken with fever and pain, his leg like a shattered stone hung to his body, heavy and useless and hurting. He remembered being taken to the marsh and fed there among the tall, bright green grass in a bright green otter holt. He had not remembered all this before. But of course, Charkky and Mikk had told him how it was; he was only remembering their tale. He looked at the crowd of curious otters splashing and pushing close to the raft and listened to Mikk tell why they had come, and he felt very silly when they rolled over in the water laughing and barking because the little band was going to steal fire.

"Not steal fire," said Mikk. "Steal the thing that makes fire."

"But who would want fire? What's it good for? Oh, humans use it in Ratnisbon, all right, but it makes such a smell."

"It's to cook food," Teb said. "I want . . ."

"He wants to cook his food," said Charkky. "He's human; his habits aren't the same as ours."

The otters went silent, staring up at Teb, thinking about this strange new idea.

"Well," said one at last, "yes, they do cook food in Ratnisbon. On the boats, too, in the harbor. You can smell it."

"But what is it that makes fire?" cried someone.

"A small flint, a little piece of metal that can strike a spark," Teb said. "Like a tiny bit of lightning. That will light the kindling, and the kindling will make the wood burn. Every soldier carries a flint," he said, puzzling that he should know this.

"You won't find much on that battlefield," said old Flokk, who was a friend of Ekkthurian's. "A band of soldiers went back and carried a wagonload away. And then the buzzards came and stayed for weeks."

"Ebis's soldiers took it all into Ratnisbon," said a pale old female with a torn ear, who was floating near the raft. "Saddles, cooking gear, blankets. They buried the dead soldiers." The Rushmarsh otters were more sophisticated than the Nightpool clan, living as they did so close to Ratnisbon. They made a hobby of watching humans, though they kept themselves hidden and secret.

Teb sighed. "It sounds as if there won't be anything left."

"Maybe," said Mikk. "Who knows what a band of soldiers might overlook?"

"There's a great cage there," said a broad-faced otter. "Big enough for ten hydruses. You wouldn't believe that men could build a cage that big, or that they would want to. Made out of whole trees, it is. We don't know what it's for, but the door to it stands wide open."

Teb frowned, puzzled. But the fleeting twinge of memory vanished into shadow and left only fear behind it. He saw Mikk watching him, and he thought Mikk guessed what he was feeling.

"There are a great many boats anchored at Cape Bay," said the Rushmarsh leader. Feskken had surfaced moments before, his pale tan coat bright amid the darker crowd. His dark muzzle made him look as if he'd had his nose in the mud. He looked Teb over. "You look much better now, boy, than last time I saw you with your leg all swollen. I expect you had all better come into Rushmarsh and wait until it grows dark to cross the bays, with all the boats about. A raft can't dive and swim underwater. Come, and take a meal with us."

So the raft was pulled into Rushmarsh along a small stream and wedged deep into the tall eelgrass. Then the otters led Teb across the marsh to their green grass holts, nearly invisible until one was right on them. Inside the largest holt, they feasted on raw oysters and shrimps and on the nutty roots of marsh lilies, which Teb found delicious.

"We have none of that at Nightpool," Mikk said. "It's one of the reasons we like to come to Rushmarsh."

"Couldn't you plant it?" Teb said. "Wouldn't it grow in the valley at Nightpool?"

The otters had never thought of such a thing.

"Why not?" said Feskken. "Great fishes, why didn't

143

anyone think of that? I'll send some youngsters at once to dig the plants up. They multiply well, we know that, for the whole south stream bed is alive with them."

"It would be better," Teb said, "to get them on our way back so they'd be fresher." He didn't know how he knew about gardening, but he did know. "They start to die the minute you pull them, and they need to have life to take root."

"I'm glad we didn't try to cross the harbors in the daytime," Mikk said. "I've never seen so many boats." The otters had a clear view of the ocean down the stream channel, though to the humans out there, looking toward the marsh, nothing was visible but a mass of green eelgrass.

"Word is," Feskken said, "that fighting in the north has driven those folk out, that the dark raiders are defeating the lands east of Chagrel. Ebis the Black has given the refugees sanctuary. They have made a large camp at the edge of the city just at the skirts of the castle."

Teb sat very still when he heard the name Ebis the Black. And when Feskken spoke of Sivich, he went chilled and thought he was really on the edge of remembering. And yet he could not remember. Mikk was watching him again, with that worried little cock of his head. Teb felt sure that when he got to the place of battle where he had been hurt, he would remember.

It was well after dark when they started out again on the sea, and Teb found the heaving ocean frightening in darkness. The raft seemed small and frail now, and where starlight touched the water, he kept watching for sharks, though the otters all said they could feel the vibrations of such creatures long before they were close.

They passed the harbors at Cape Bay and the Bay of Fear, and in both bays they could see in the starlight rows and rows of boats of all kinds and sizes anchored and tied one to another. On some, lamps burned, though most were dark and quiet. They could smell meat cooking, which made Teb wild with desire, and the scent of frying onions was nearly more than he could stand.

Beyond the Bay of Fear the coast belonged to Baylentha, and they reached the scene of battle near to midnight. There they came ashore and curled down among the heavy marsh grasses to sleep. A smell of death clung to the place, and Teb lay awake a long time.

The knowledge of himself was here, and he thought if he could go to sleep in just the right way, he would wake in the morning knowing who he was, knowing why he had been in this battle. Maybe he was a refugee, like the people on the boats.

But when he woke at dawn he didn't know any more than he had the night before. The sky was barely light, like tarnished silver, and the hills in the south and west black silhouettes. He looked up across the marsh to the battlefield and saw the huge, towering cage.

It was immense, made of whole trees, just as the

otters had said, and held together with chain as big as a man's leg. Its door was propped open, and he knew he had been in there, and he rose and began to walk toward it almost as if he walked in a dream, stepping around the still-sleeping otters, who lay curled together in a silky brown tangle.

The battlefield was strewn with the bleached skeletons of horses. They were grisly in their broken helplessness, their wild spirits fled, their lovely warm, moving bodies gone, their collapsing bones sinking now into the earth, their eye sockets empty and their brains eaten away, and whatever else it was that had made those wild spirits all vanished. The smell of death and rotting meat lingered, and here and there a hank of hide and hair still clung to the bone. A few saddles lay broken beneath the bodies, though most had been taken away. As Teb stared around him, a ghost of the battle touched him, distant shouting and the thunder of hooves and the clashing of swords rang in his head, then was stilled, and he could not make the battle come clear; but his fear had increased, so he was sweating and cold. And a song of the skeletons and of death formed quickly and harshly, with a stark white beauty.

There were no skeletons of men. He looked for the mound of a common grave, but saw none.

He approached the cage and stood looking, and knew he should remember this. He stared inside at the earth, striped with the shadows of the great bars, and almost knew. Almost. There had been terror in that cage.

And wonder. It was gone now. He turned away at last, strangely lonely, and began to prowl among the tangled heaps of bones, trying not to think of them as horses.

He found a rusted knife in a patch of weed between the bodies and thought it would be fine when it was polished. He found a single boot and let it lie. He saw the paw prints of foxes crossing the battlefield, marked over with hoof prints, and he stood looking at them, puzzling.

Why would fox prints stir him? Why was he so sure they were foxes?

He glanced toward the cage, then toward the grass where the otters slept. He wished they would wake and come to keep him company. But the sky had grown orange with sunrise before he saw Mikk rear up out of the grass to look around him, then soon Charkky, then the others. He grinned and felt better when they came across the battlefield, hah-hahing, to help him search.

They quartered the battlefield back and forth, the otters rummaging around the heaps of bones, soon making a game of it. They chased one another in and out among the skeletons, picking up useless objects— a thrown horseshoe, a broken bridle rein—and stopped to eat the blackberries that grew along the edge of the marsh. Teb listened to their huffing laughter and shook his head and kept searching, though he was growing discouraged.

147

But then at last, in a small ravine that pushed back against the rising hills, he found a leather pack down among the thick bushes. He pulled it out, undid the strings, and spilled the contents onto the ground.

There was a pair of brown socks with a hole in one toe. A pair of linen drawers for a very big man. Another knife, not so rusted. A twist of tobacco. A sewing kit—needle and thread and scissors—in a little cloth bag. And something dried that might once have been cheese, for it had stained the leather and cloth with its oil. He put the socks and knife and sewing kit in the pack and left the rest. There was no flint, so he kept searching, though in the end it was Jukka who found it as she rummaged into a tangle of blackberries. She found the flint and played with it, ate some berries, then at last came loping up the hills to Teb to ask if this might be what he searched for, this little unimportant-looking bit of metal in the wire holder, with the second piece of metal dangling from it by a chain.

Teb took it from her and gathered some dry grass into a pile, then struck the metals. The sparks made Jukka back off in alarm, huffing at him. The others gathered at once as he got the tiny fire smoldering.

"Hah," said Charkky. "It smells bad. No wonder we never had any."

"On Nightpool," Mikk said, "you'd best do this where old Ekkthurian can't smell it."

But to Teb the fire smelled wonderful, and he felt

disappointed that the others found it useless and silly. They gave it another look, then went off again playing among the nut grass and blackberry bushes. Teb dropped the flint into his pack, and snuffed out the tiny fire reluctantly. It was much later, when he had stopped to eat some blackberries for his breakfast, that he found the bow, tangled down among the blackberry vines.

It was a good bow, made of oak, but broken. He wondered if he could mend it. He went back among the skeletons to pick up arrows, and soon had ten, then fourteen, that he thought he might use if he sharpened the steel tips and replaced the feathers. He showed the otters how it would shoot once he repaired it, and this impressed them far more than the fire.

"How far will the arrows go?" Charkky said.

"Oh, maybe clear to the hills, if I fix it right."

Mikk examined the bow, the curves so perfectly formed, the little notches where the bowstring would fasten.

"It would be fine for rabbit," Teb said.

"Yes, and for shooting sharks from the bank," Mikk said. "Could you do that?"

"I could try. I could learn to." Why not? He wasn't sure how to mend the bow, but he guessed he would think of a way. He had gone to scavenge some strips of leather when Kkelpin came clumsily dragging an iron cookpot.

149

"Is this of any use? It might make a good bowl for clams."

"Oh, it's more than a bowl. I can cook in it. It's perfect. And it will fit in the pack, I think." It was not a very large pot and was coated with dirt and ashes. He brushed it off and rearranged the pack so it fit, then went with Kkelpin back to the site of the camp cookfire, but there were no other prizes; it had all been taken away. There should be a big iron grid, he thought, then puzzled that he knew nothing more, was still puzzling over a fleeting vision of men around the cook-fire as they set out for home in late afternoon, the bow and arrows across his knees, and the pack strapped to his waist with a bit of bridle rein. How could he know something down inside but not remember it? What would it take to make him remember who he was and why he had been here? And why did the great cage make him feel so strange?

He watched the sea roll green, shot with light in the afternoon sun, the dark otter bodies flashing beneath the glassy water and dark faces bobbing up to stare at him with laughing eyes, and at last he forgot his own puzzling for the joyous games of the otters. They passed the crowded harbors well after dusk and slipped into Rushmarsh, the raft churning and rocking in the busy water as a crowd of otters dove and played around it in greeting.

But this was more than joyous greeting; there was something wrong. The plunging agitation of the Rush-

marsh otters soon infected the six, and from the raft
Teb strained to make sense of the tangle of words as
everyone talked at once.

"There has been something in the sea," said Feskken, swimming up to the raft. "Something huge and
unfamiliar." His dark muzzle pointed off toward the
darkening horizon, as the old pale female joined him.

"It came to the mouth of the bay," she said. "It was
thrashing and churning out there, and then lay still
for a long time, as if it were watching us."

"It stayed until the sun went down," Feskken said;
"then it sank deep, too deep for us to feel its vibrations.
Maybe it went away, maybe not. You had best spend
the night in Rushmarsh."

12

❈

"It wasn't a whale?" Charkky said as he settled down in Feskken's holt. The grass house was larger than those around it and crowded now to bursting with the otters of Rushmarsh and the six from Nightpool, and Teb, as well as a gaggle of cubs. Teb sat near the door, where he could slip out to tend his fire.

"Not a whale?" Mikk repeated. "A lone bull, following krill?"

"We don't think it was a whale," said Feskken. "It's the wrong time of year for a whale to come in so close, near to Rushmarsh. There was nothing to draw it, no krill in the water."

Teb was glad they weren't out on the dark sea now, with an unknown creature lurking. He rose and left the otters and went to the old abandoned grass holt where he had built his fire, and sat hunkered before it, cheered by the burning driftwood and the boiling iron pot. He dropped in some wild onion, and that smelled grand, then the shellfish and lily roots. And then he sat alone, opening the steamed clams and oysters and stuffing himself nearly to sickness. Nothing had ever tasted so good, juicy, and hot, and the flavors of seafood and lily roots a hundredfold richer than ever they could be raw. He was almost finished when Charkky and Jukka and Kkelpin came to sniff the cooked shellfish, but only Charkky would try it. The other two watched him with distaste.

"It isn't bad," Charkky announced. But he didn't take a second helping.

Jukka just looked at him. Kkelpin's whiskers twitched with amusement. Later when Teb yawned and yawned and couldn't keep his eyes open, no otter would come to sleep beside his fire, so he bedded down in the fresh rushes alone, feeling very cozy, and dreamed of building a fire pit in his cave. He woke to such brilliant red light he thought the holt had caught fire, but it was only the sunrise. They were off before breakfast, the little raft loaded, now, with a great hank of freshly dug lilies, dirt still clinging to the roots, and barely room for Teb to crowd aboard. Once out of Rushmarsh, he swam for a long way, keeping a wary eye on the open sea, then climbed back on the raft to warm in the rising sun. He was glad the weather had warmed; he would not be swimming in the winter, for already

the sea had turned chill. He thought of getting his
tunic out of the pack, then didn't, and was almost
asleep when suddenly the raft was rocking and the sea
heaving as the otters raced with it toward the cliffs.

"Jump, Tebriel! Jump for the cliff!" Charkky shouted
as a monstrous black shape foamed out of the sea,
nearly on them. "Jump!"

He leaped for the cliff and clung, and climbed as the
raft crashed against it and foam spewed below him;
he prayed the otters were climbing, too. He slipped,
snatched at wet rock, and nearly fell. Then the monster
was beneath him, huge, storming at the cliff so the
stone shook. Teb heaved upward, tearing his hands,
and didn't know afterward how he had moved so fast.

He stood atop the cliff staring around for the otters
as the monster thrashed and heaved below: a giant
three-headed sea hydrus. He backed away from the
edge as it reared toward him; then he spun away and
found a sharp stone, and wished he had a knife. But
the pack was lost, and all in it. Down to his right, the
raft had broken apart, and its logs were pounding in
the waves that beat against the cliff. There was no
sign of the otters, either on the cliff or in the sea. The
creature remained still for a minute, looking, and then
it thrashed up against the cliff again, rising higher in
a spray of foam, the water pouring down its broad
black body, and its necks stretched out so the three
heads came over the top as he fled backward, each

head as big as a pony, the faces terrible parodies of human faces.

The muzzles were longer than a man's, the mouths broader, and the teeth close together and pointed. The eyes were men's eyes, muddy gray and vicious, three sets of identical eyes watching and watching him with cold malice as he stood crouched, knowing it couldn't climb, yet ready to run if it did, and to fight if it overtook him. The protruding mouths grinned and drooled, and the center one licked evilly. It wanted him—he could see it in its eyes, could feel its desire for him. An emptiness came in his mind as he watched it, as if something had been taken from him.

It watched Teb for a long time. It knew something he didn't know, seeing him from some incalculable distance in time and space, Teb thought, and the emptiness within him grew, and the terror. Had it killed the otters? He felt sick, for surely it had killed them; and yet he was so very drawn to the creature, and wanted, in some incredibly sick way, to walk those few steps to the cliff edge, into its horrible reach. It looked at him for so long, he was cold and hot all at once, and then it smiled, all three faces smiled the same knowing, promising smile.

Then it sank down away into the sea.

Teb stood on the cliff's edge, faint and sick, staring down at the empty sea. Blood flowed down his chest. He watched the sea and prayed that a brown head

155

would pop up, and another, prayed for the otters with clenched fists; and the sea remained empty. His mind was filled with them, with their sleek bodies flashing through the sea, their laughing faces and dripping whiskers and their laughing dark eyes. He watched the sea for a long, long time, searching close in, far out among the waves, seeing only emptiness, staring down along the empty rocky cliff. Then at last he turned away, stricken with a cold, terrible grieving.

But he had gone only a few steps when loud splashing made him turn back to stare over the edge, and he saw the hydrus thrashing deep below the surface; white foam spewed up, its dark shadow lurched and twisted, and then the foam turned red.

It lurched to the surface and black shadows moved below it; one immense head thrashed up out of the waves, then the second, bleeding below the left eye. The third head surfaced in a pool of foaming blood, its throat slashed open.

The hydrus turned in its own blood, floundering. It moved out across the sea trailing red, and soon it was only a huge black shadow like the shadow of a fast-moving cloud.

Teb stood staring long after it vanished and its blood had washed away in the sea. A huffing sigh made him turn, and there was Litta, erect on her hind legs, gazing at him with laughing brown eyes.

In her paw she held the rusty knife. He grabbed her and hugged her, fishy breath and all.

And when she led him to the cliff, there they all were, five brown heads bobbing, their whiskers dripping as they stared up at him with huge grins. Litta handed him the knife, then scurried down to them.

Teb followed, and when at last he stood on the narrow beach the otters leaped out of the surf to push against him, laughing. Charkky stood up to touch his face. "Hah, Teb," he said, grinning. "You escaped. You cut your chin, though."

"It's almost stopped bleeding. I thought the hydrus ate you."

"And we hoped it didn't eat *you*," said Charkky.

"But what happened?" Then Teb saw the leather pack, and the bundle of lilies beside it.

"Kkelpin grabbed the pack as it was sinking," Mikk said. "There are caves down there with air pockets. We laid the pack out and found the knives. We've never used knives, only sharp shells. The knives saved us. A hydrus doesn't much like to be hurt, to be bleeding in the sea. Maybe the sharks will finish it off."

"And," Jukka said, "the lilies got lodged on a crevice down below the underwater caves. The bow and arrows, though—"

"It ate them," interrupted Litta. "It grabbed them and crunched them down."

"Maybe it thought they were eels," said Hokki, giggling.

"Maybe it knew they were weapons," Charkky said, "and didn't want us to have them."

"Does it know that much?" Teb said. But of course the hydrus knew, more than Teb could guess, knew deep things that made him shiver. He looked out seaward, fear catching up with him now, then looked down the coast toward Nightpool. The island itself could not be seen for the jutting of the point at Jade Beach. The otters knew what he was thinking, that he didn't want to get back in the water, was thinking of his legs dangling below the surface, where anything could grab them.

"You can walk along the shore over the rocks," Mikk said.

"I will walk with you," said Charkky. "We'll have to take to the sea when we get beyond Jade Beach, or go over the point; the cliff falls away there steep and slick."

Teb tied the pack to his waist and shouldered the lilies, and they started out, Mikk galumphing ahead of him and the other five diving swiftly seaward deep down, then up and down along the surface, playing in the sea as if they had quite forgotten the hydrus.

"How do they know it won't come back?" Teb asked.

"They don't. But you can't be afraid all the time. Your chin's bleeding again; press some seaweed to it."

As they traveled, Teb tried to tell himself one of the songs that had come to him so strangely, yet he found he couldn't. They were all gone suddenly, not one word would come back, though they had all been there before the hydrus. They were the only real memories he had. And they had seemed to him more than memories, too. They had seemed a powerful link to someone else and to what his future held. They had seemed to him a kind of talisman, a prediction, just as Thakkur's visions were predictions. Now they were gone, the last thread with himself broken.

He followed Charkky in silence, feeling lost and afraid. He hadn't very much more to take away. Had the hydrus done this, reached him in the most private, safest place he had? They made their way up the cliff so they could cross the point at Jade Beach rather than going in the water. Just as they reached the cliff top, a wind and darkness swept out of the sky filled with the dusty smell of feathers, and a huge owl came swooping across the top of his head, giant wings beating at him. Teb ducked as the dark bird banked in front of him, staring into his face with fierce yellow eyes; its screaming cry stopped his heart as it hovered over him; an owl as big as an otter and seeming twice that with its wings spread. Its red beak opened cruelly.

Then it laughed. A harsh, guttural laugh. It landed before him and folded its wings, and stared at him fierce as sin.

Charkky stood ready to run, but Teb just stared, because something about an owl made him feel comfortable, even though this owl was far from comforting.

Its stomach feathers were buff, but the rest of it was nearly black, mottled with flecks of rust. Its red beak was sharply curved, and its great ears extended to the sides of its head as if it were wearing a hat. Its voice was gravelly and hissing.

"Have you seen the black monster in the sea? Hydrus! I am searching for the hydrus. Three heads. Faces like men. I have been tracking it for weeks."

"We've seen it," Charkky said, cross from being frightened. "What have you to do with such a thing? Certainly you have no better manners than it has, swooping down on a person."

The owl grinned and bowed, which only made Charkky scowl harder. "I follow the hydrus to learn its ways. Where it is bound. It moves ahead of the armies of darkness. Quazelzeg is its master. It drowns men by swamping boats, and it loves only darkness."

"It attacked us," Charkky said, studying the owl with curiosity. "We wounded it, and it went away deeper into the sea. Back there." He pointed. "Just off the last point."

The owl snapped its wings open and crouched to leap skyward.

"Wait," Charkky cried. "You have something to tell of the hydrus. Thakkur will want to hear it."

"Can't wait. I must follow. I will return if I can, but now I must follow. . . ." He leaped then, with one whish of air and then in silence as he rose on the sea wind, and Teb watched him grow smaller as he sped east toward the open sea.

And inside Teb's head the owl's words echoed:

". . . it loves only darkness. . . . I must follow." And it was as if those same words echoed in his own spirit and he, too, must, at some time near, follow the hydrus, follow darkness.

13

It was spring before the owl returned. They did not see the hydrus again, though a watch was kept at all times from the high ridge above Thakkur's cave. Winter settled in early and fierce, cutting the warm autumn away with sheets of blizzard-cold wind, and the seas grew huge and pounding, so all the otters, even Thakkur, moved out of the seaward caves into those overlooking the inner valley.

Teb moved into Charkky and Mikk's cave, bringing his new gull-feather blanket, to the envy of both otters. On the coldest nights they all three slept under it. He supposed he smelled as fishy now as the otters did, though he was still aware of their fishy breath at night. It was nice sleeping close to their warm, silky smoothness, and they were all three cozy and snug even on the stormiest nights. Both Charkky and Mikk had come to like cooked shellfish, and the three of them made their fires on the little beach below the south cliff where the waves rolled by at an angle. Hardly anyone came there. Twice a day they boiled up a succulent meal in the black iron pot. But it was here that Ekkthurian and Gorkk and Urikk appeared suddenly one evening from around the bend of the cliff, their black eyes flashing with fury and their teeth bared.

"I thought I smelled a stench," said Ekkthurian. "Fire! It is fire! A vile human habit. And what are you two doing, Charkky and Mikk? One might expect it of a human, but young otters do not play with fire."

"We are cooking supper," said Mikk evenly. "Go away."

Charkky stared at Mikk, amazed. It was not the custom to be rude to your elders. And then, taking heart from Mikk, Charkky showed his teeth to the sour old otter and gave him a low, angry growl.

"Thakkur said we could cook here," Teb said. "He said I could make a fire."

Ekkthurian scowled at the three of them and began to kick sand into the fire and the cookpot. Teb watched their meal ruined and did nothing. It was not his place, as an outsider, to defy Ekkthurian. He kept his anger in check with great effort, even when the thin otter turned on him with lips drawn back, his eyes slitted and his ears laid flat to his head. "Not only do you make fire, human boy, you bring other evil as well."

"What evil?" Teb stood his ground, daring Ekkthurian to bite him.

"You have brought human weapons to Nightpool. Not only knives, but you assist the otters themselves in making a bow. It is against the ways of the animals to have such things."

All three stared. How did Ekkthurian know? Mikk had found a fine piece of oak washed onto the beach, and they had, indeed, been carving out a bow and fashioning shell tips for arrows, the two otters working carefully at this new skill and very pleased with themselves.

"The bow isn't hurting you; it might even help you someday," Mikk said reasonably. "And the fires don't hurt you, either. Why can't you leave Teb alone?"

"He does not belong here. No human belongs here. He has turned Thakkur's mind. Thakkur had no business allowing him in Nightpool."

Teb stared at Ekkthurian, then turned away and emptied his cookpot onto the fire, drowning the flame and ruining their supper. Then he climbed the cliff beside Charkky and Mikk.

They ate raw food that night. But the next day, at Thakkur's direction, they built their fire right on the ledge below the cave and cooked their supper there before a ring of curious, arguing otters. And it was then that two factions began to grow, one fanned by Ekkthurian's fury, the other angered by his interference, until all over the island, otters were arguing.

Teb supposed Ekkthurian's little group had a right to be critical if they wished. But did they have a right to try to turn others against him?

"It will pass," Mitta said. "Thakkur will deal with it."

But it doesn't take many folk to make misery when they speak with hatred. Teb and Charkky and Mikk and the younger otters kept more and more to themselves, and this did not please Thakkur. He did not want the island divided. Then the owl returned, and for a while the quarrel was forgotten.

With the coming of spring the colony had moved back into the caves on the outer rim, and though Teb missed Charkky and Mikk, it was nice to have solitude, too. The owl came swooping directly in from the sea one evening, dropping low along the cliff like a great black shadow, to darken the cliffside doorways and startle the otters at supper. His scream brought them out onto the ledge, staring. Teb had been sewing a pair of sharkskin flippers, fitting them to his feet, and he jammed the needle into his finger hard when the first cry came. He ran out to see the red-beaked old fellow flapping and scolding at a band of strapping cubs that were leaping along the ledge after him, huffing and swearing. The owl banked again, saw Teb, and turned back to land on Teb's shoulder, almost throwing him down the cliff. The young otters were on Teb at once, clambering up his legs to get at it, shouting words Teb didn't know they knew. Farther along the ledge he could see the white otter emerge.

"There he is," shouted the owl. "It's Thakkur I want to see." He swept away, and Teb followed, running, and at Thakkur's cave, the owl flew straight in and landed on a high shelf, his great ears straight out with anger as he stared down at the clambering youngsters who had followed. Thakkur stood looking up at him, his whiskers twitching with amusement.

The owl glared. "Your young haven't any manners at all. I didn't know otters could swear like that."

"They can when they think the clan is threatened," Thakkur said. "You must be Red Unat. I have heard of you. Old Bloody Beak, I've heard you called."

The owl's ears twitched. He scowled at Thakkur, then opened his beak in what might be a smile, though it looked more as if he would eat Thakkur. "Old Bloody Beak it is, Thakkur of Nightpool. And I have heard a tale or two about you."

Otters had gathered thick in the cave. Charkky pushed close to Teb, his whiskers stiff with interest.

"Did you find the hydrus?" Thakkur asked. "Did it die from the wounds our otters gave it?"

"I tracked it by disturbances among the fishes, a great empty swath and the little fish all adither on both sides. I tracked it to Mernmeth, and there was blood on the waters there."

"Mernmeth," Charkky whispered to Teb, "is a drowned city north and east, where a great shallow runs out."

"Did it die there?" asked Thakkur.

"It is still alive. It thrashed in agony, but it lived. I watched and patroled the coast, very hard work in the icy weather. When it emerged again in dead winter, I followed it.

"It went north. It has been attacking the harbors along the Benaynne Archipelago, where Quazelzeg's armies are raiding. It prevents escape by water, and Quazelzeg has taken many slaves and murdered hundreds."

"I am sorry to hear that," said Thakkur. "Though it is not unexpected."

"If the dark raiders are not stopped," said Red Unat, "no one will be safe from them. They are not men, and are much more dangerous than humans. Quazelzeg and those closest to him are, in truth, the unliving, dedicated to anything that negates life, that defiles and destroys the strength of life."

Teb stood tense. All of this was so very familiar, and yet still the dark emptiness lay in his mind.

"At some point," said Red Unat, "the animals must join against Quazelzeg. It is inevitable. The great cats and wolves, and the foxes, perhaps even unicorns, though they have disappeared from this hemisphere into the elfin lands. But mark you, the animals must join forces. Already there is talk of such things." He settled more comfortably on his perch and fluffed his feathers. Thakkur sat up straighter on his sleeping bench, his broad white tail stretched along it, his front paws together, his whiskers stiff as he stared up at Red Unat.

"There is a resistance army growing among the humans," the owl said. "But Quazelzeg is powerful, more powerful than many understand.

"He took five hundred hostages at Mevidin and is forcing them to serve as soldiers and camp slaves, even the small girls. He has divided his forces into three bands to drive wedges down into the Nasden Confederacy, and he strips the fields of food for his own forces, leaving the cities and villages to starve."

Teb listened for a long time, sick at the talk and agitated with his own inner turmoil as memories tried to push out. That night his dreams were filled with wings. With the owl's swooping wings, and with the fluttering wings of a tiny owl as it flew to his shoulder and whispered some message to him. He also dreamt of the heavy, dark wings of slavering jackals, as the creatures snarled and flapped around his face.

Then came wings so huge, so bright and glowing, that they were like pearl-tinted clouds descending. He reached out to them laughing, and the dragon looked down at him, her long green eyes lit with some wonderful message. Then fires came in his dreams. The hearth fire in a tapestried room, a cookfire surrounded by soldiers. Fires and wings twisted together, and there were faces. A red-haired man and an old graying man, and the face of a girl, golden and smiling.

He woke.

And he remembered.

Dawn had barely come, the sky and sea deep gray. He lay looking at the pale lines of waves, remembering it all, his father's murder before his eyes in the hall, his mother's drowning, his own enslavement, and Blaggen and the stinking jackals. His journey tied to the horse like a sack of meal, his escape with Garit and Pakkna. Nison-Serth and the foxes, the dear foxes.

The cage, and the dragon tearing at his chains, pulling them free, and searing them from his legs with her hot breath. He remembered running and dodging between racing horsemen, being snatched up by a horseman on a white mount, then falling. . . .

Then nothing, until he woke bobbing on the sea, soaking from the waves, the pain in his leg terrible. And Charkky's and Mikk's wet, concerned frowns.

He sat thinking for a long time, and then went along the cliff to Thakkur's cave. He found the white otter making a meal of periwinkles and sea urchin roe that one of the cubs had brought him. He sat down quietly.

The white otter's dark eyes looked him over. Teb looked back, filled with news. And with questions.

Thakkur finished the roe and rose to toss the shells into the sea; then he turned again to Teb. "You remember," he said simply. "I see it in your face. You remember." His dark eyes were filled with kindness and with wisdom.

"Yes, I remember. I dreamt, then woke remembering. So strange. How could I have forgotten it all?

Even my sister?" The cool sea wind touched him as it circled Thakkur's cave. He stared at Thakkur's dark, caring eyes. "I am Tebriel, son of the murdered King of Auric. My father was killed by Sivich of the dark raiders. My mother drowned in the Bay of Dubla."

They talked for a long time. Teb told Thakkur all that had happened on the journey to Baylentha, and much that happened before. He told a great deal about his mother, and once he felt tears start, but he choked them back. He told about the little owl carrying messages to Camery. And that Sivich intended to use Camery for breeding. Thakkur listened. But he offered no answers.

"I must leave Nightpool now. I must help Camery; somehow I must get her away from Sivich."

Thakkur said nothing for a long time. He moved about the cave, looking out at the sea, rearing up to touch objects along the shelves. Then he dropped to all fours, and flowed up into his sleeping shelf, his movements liquid and graceful, from his broad white tail to his black nose and eyes.

"I expect the owl will return very soon," he said, rearing up on his sleeping shelf to stare at Teb. "You would do better to wait for him. He will have more news of Auric, for he goes to seek out the underground armies that are said to be based at Bleven."

"Bleven is where Garit sent me."

"Yes. It is possible your friend Garit has already rescued Camery. The owl could learn whether she is still in the tower and save you possible capture. It would be no trick for him to drop down into the tower at night and never wake the jackals."

Teb knew that Thakkur was right, though all his anger at Sivich, all his instincts, tried to drive him out at once to attack the palace at Auric. But alone? What could he do alone?

"If you go now and are killed or taken captive again," Thakkur said reasonably, "what good will that do your sister? And what help will that be to Auric, or to the forces that fight the dark?"

"What *is* the dark? I know what the foxes told me, that it is the unliving, that it—" Teb stopped abruptly, staring at Thakkur. "That it takes your memory away," he said slowly. "Gone—they showed me, Renata showed me. It was like what I felt. Exactly."

Thakkur looked back at him.

"Did the dark do that to me?"

The white otter shook his head. "I cannot tell, Tebriel. There are other things that make one's memory fail. Injury, severe sickness. You cannot be certain it was the dark."

The white otter moved, gliding across the cave and back restlessly. They could hear the laughter of a band of young otters playing in the waves. When Thakkur spoke again, it was sadly.

"You cannot know for certain. You cannot know precisely what the dark is, either, Tebriel, until you can know the turnings of Tirror's past. Few on Tirror remember, yet only through understanding how Tirror was born can one understand the dark."

"Tell me, then. Will you tell me?"

Thakkur settled onto his shelf and folded one paw over the other. And as he began the tale of Tirror, pictures came in Teb's mind of all Thakkur told him, and of more, as if Thakkur's words unlocked stores of knowledge in his own mind, hidden and surprising.

"Tirror was born a spinning ball of gases," Thakkur said, "a ball of gases formed by a hand of such power that no creature can know its true nature, the power of the Graven Light. The ball spun and cooled to molten fire, then over centuries it turned to barren stone. All by design, Tebriel. It warped and twisted into mountains and valleys, but there was no tree or plant, no animal, no water to nurture life. Then the power of the Graven Light covered the barren, cooling world with clouds, and the clouds gave down water, and then life came. Small at first, then richer, more varied, until all Tirror knew creatures and plants and abundance.

"But from the very beginning, the fire and bareness and the promise of life lured the dark that always exists in black space, and that luring was not by design. The dark crept through crevices into the molten stone, and it lay dormant through all the changes, and even the power that made Tirror could not rout it. It insinuated itself into each new form the land took. And it waited. It is the opposite to the force of light that created Tirror, and perhaps for this reason it could not be routed. It is malevolent, it is thirsty, and it lay accumulating self-knowledge and earth-knowledge."

Teb shivered. "And the light couldn't drive it out?"

"The light *did* nothing."

"But . . ."

"Perhaps it is a part of the pattern, that the dark be here. That it works its own forces and its own tests upon Tirror's life. I don't know, Tebriel. I know a soul can find true life or fall dying, according to whether it embraces the dark." The white otter took up a small round stone and held it quietly, as if it soothed him. "Humans don't remember, as they once did, the long-shadowed tale of this world, or even that there was a time before the small island countries existed. They don't remember the five huge continents that once were the only land on Tirror."

Teb tried to imagine huge continents, and no island nations, but could not. "How could that be? What happened to them?"

"Those five continents were drowned. The small island continents are the highest mountains of those vast lands; they are all that remains above water.

"Once there were great ice caps on Tirror, but then the weather grew warmer. The ice began to melt and flood the seas. The seas rose and flooded the land, and drowned the lowlands and the valleys and all the cities there. It did not happen quickly; the shores crept up and up, and folk moved slowly back. But many starved when the crop lands and pastures were covered."

"How could people forget such a thing? How long ago?"

"Perhaps twenty generations. Humans have forgotten because the source of their world memory is all but gone.

"Once this knowledge was relived in every village, in every place where men and animals met, in ceremonies in the old temple sanctuaries. The past was brought alive by the skill of the singing dragons and the dragonbards, by the wonder of the dragon song. . . ."

A strange feeling gripped Teb, a sense of power that puzzled him, and he saw his hands were shaking and clasped them tight.

"But the force of the dark grew stronger, until at last it drove the dragons out, and captured or killed the bards. And the dark spread tales about the dragon song until soon folk no longer believed in it. And then, at last, it seemed there were no more dragons, not anywhere on Tirror. Memory died. And with its death, each person was separated from the rich multitude of the past, and was alone. Without memory, Tebriel, we cannot know what the present means. We cannot understand evil, or goodness. Our world is caught in despair. Perhaps it was the scent of despair that drew a more powerful dark to us, that drew the unliving into Tirror from far worlds.

"In the far north," Thakkur said, "lies a black palace that once was hidden beneath the ice. Where it came from, no one knows. When the ice melted, it stood alone there, and it is girded with uncounted doors, and each door leads to a world beyond this world.

"It is believed that Quazelzeg came from there and brought the sea hydrus, and brought a terrible lust to join with the dark of Tirror. And that is when the dark began to rise and create forces to crush all world memory, bringing despair, and so in the end crushing all life except that which it will enslave."

"He brought the sea hydrus," Teb said. And he could feel again the creature's dark evil. "It made a blackness in my mind. It destroyed . . . something I did remember. I thought, when I looked at it, that it . . . wanted to possess me."

There was a long silence between them, in which, it seemed to Teb, questions and answers and knowledge passed back and forth, things Thakkur was unwilling to speak of, things subtle and secret and not to be spoken of, yet.

"It may well have wanted to possess you, Tebriel." They stared at each other.

After a long time, Thakkur said, "It is told that, once, the dark leaders trained the hydrus to drive out and kill the singing dragons. Dark soldiers used to capture the baby singing dragons when they flew tame and gentle into the cities, and they put them into a pit with a hydrus. The babies would stand up on their hind legs and try to sing—until the hydrus tore out their throats."

14

It takes ten months to hatch a dragon. The eggs were cream colored and rubbery. By the time the dragonlings hatched in late spring, the shells were stained dark by the rotted carcasses. Dawncloud would lay her head close to each egg and listen to the new little creature inside, wriggling and changing position. When the first hatchling began to scratch on the egg, during a screaming storm that nearly tore the nest from the stony peak, Dawncloud hunkered down over it and cocked her great head, and smiled, filled with wonder and joy, then raised her face to the raging skies and screamed her pleasure out onto the storm.

By the time spring had raged its final storm and turned gentle, all five young were out of the egg and curling and twisting about the nest, raising their little heads up blindly into the warm spring light. In another ten days their eyes were open and they had begun to perch out on the edge of the nest flapping their young wings, and to cluster around Dawncloud, slithering up her sides and listening intently to the songs she sang to them. She had sung to the eggs, too, all during the incubation, and now the dragonlings pushed at her with demanding little horns to hear the songs again, and to hear others. Without the songs, a dragonling is nothing; the songs were as much a part of them as their brand-new fangs and their fiery breath.

They were very alike, these young, yet each was its own creature, bold in its own way, clever in its own way. They named themselves, as is the custom among dragons, with names chosen from the wealth of the songs. Three were females; two were males. The males would grow darker later. They were heavier and broader of head. The males named themselves Starpounder and Nightraider. The females were Windcaller, Moon-song, and Seastrider. It was Seastrider who began to yearn first out toward the vast world of Tirror, to lean out on the winds staring eastward as if something drew her there, where the sea lay beyond Windthorst. As the summer grew warm they all began to flap on the edge of the nest, and then in late summer to soar down to the lower peaks. Dawncloud was very protective of them, for fear of common dragons and hydrus, and would not let them fly out over the bays at all, for fear of the more formidable sea hydrus she knew lurked somewhere there.

She had sensed the hydrus during all her long months on the nest, and sometimes an ugly song of him touched her. It was not a good time on Tirror; the dark was growing bold. And the young humans who could turn the tide were not many. One boy, one girl, and if there were others they were distant, and vague in her mind.

She did not know just where the boy and girl were, but not far. Surely on, or near to, Windthorst. The wild, larger scenes that marked Tirror's history filled her mind now, the battles and movements of armies, perhaps because of the growing warfare that scoured this world, and it was harder to touch the unique, small scenes and thoughts. The boy's songs touched her sometimes, though, pleasing her and exciting Sea-strider unbearably. Did the boy sense the young dragon's yearning? Was he even aware of her?

Dawncloud herself had begun to know a yearning, as fragile as mist, so small a feeling that she could hardly trust it. Was there to be another bonding for her? She had not heard her own name spoken by a human voice since her tall, sandy-haired bard, Daban, had leaped to her back for the last time calling her name and laughing with her and singing. When Daban was murdered she flew to Tendreth Slew and crawled into the mud and went to sleep there, heartbroken.

Was there another calling now?

Did someone stand at the doors of the black palace, perhaps, come from another world? Or was someone meant to come to those dark doors soon, approaching the vague gauze of Tirror's future? From no other place, she thought, would the sense come, then vanish so elusively. It was a woman, she thought. But the pale aura of her presence was so very faint, nearly without substance at all.

Dawncloud was far too busy tending her young to dwell long on her own needs, for she was driven to hunt ever harder to feed the rapacious young fledglings, to sing to them long into the night, and to watch over their still-clumsy flying. Starpounder still held his tail too low in the wind and grappled at the nest before launching out in unsteady flight; his three sisters laughed at him before leaping skyward themselves. Nightraider kept to himself, diligently strengthening his wings. It took the males longer to master flight because of their added weight. But summer was young yet; they would all be skilled by fall.

The owl returned to Nightpool after the last spring blizzard, and then again two days later. When he learned that Teb was the son of the murdered king of Auric, he flew at once to Auric's palace to search for Camery, but within two days was back, to say she was not in the tower.

"Did you look for her in Bleven?" Teb said, his heart sinking. "Maybe Garit took her to Bleven."

"I went to Bleven to the place of brewing, as you said. Ah, fine brew, such as was left. There wasn't much, an open crock, and the brewer himself gone, no sign of anyone, the place ransacked and the whole town deserted."

"And Camery was gone?"

"Yes. If she was ever there."

"And you didn't see a redheaded man?"

"I saw no one."

"I must go to look for her."

"Where will you look that the animals cannot? Already the foxes search for her up through Mithlan and Baylentha and over into Ratnisbon. The foxes send you greeting, Tebriel. Did you know that Luex and Faxel tried to rescue you there on the battlefield at Baylentha and drove the dying horse off your leg?"

"No. I don't remember. . . . But what happened to them? It must have been their cries that Charkky and Mikk heard."

"Chased by jackals clear to the western ridge, where they went to ground and lost them," Old Bloody Beak said, grinning. And then, "Here," he said, pushing out a small object that had lain under his feathered posterior where he had dropped it. "I found this in the house of the brewer, underneath a girl's ragged gown and tangled beneath a pile of bedclothes."

Teb took the small, leather-bound diary eagerly. It was Camery's, the spine sewn with linen thread by a little girl's hand, the vellum pages covered with her neat, familiar handwriting. She *had* been at Bleven!

He turned the pages, hoping they would speak to him. But he could read no word, only a few scattered letters and his own name. The writing was very small and crowded, and she had written on both sides of the paper. The last entry was hastily written, scrawled angling across the page.

"I can't read it," Teb said, ashamed. "Can you?"

"No owl can read. Our eyes are not suited to such work. Nor can otters," he said, anticipating Teb's thought. "Owls can see small birds at great distances, and an otter can see clearly underwater. But letters on a page are altogether a different matter."

"I *must* know what it says. Maybe the last pages tell what has happened to her."

He put the diary into his tunic pocket. He would not look at it again until after the meeting in the great cave, where Thakkur bid the owl come for prayer.

Teb sat at the side of the cave with Charkky and Mikk and Jukka and Kkelpin, ignoring the sour looks from Ekkthurian's friends. More otters than not smiled at him, twitching their whiskers, and he heard soft hahs across the cave in gentle greeting. The owl sat up on the dais next to Thakkur, surrounded by the twelve, Ekkthurian scowling among them, along with Urikk and Gorkk.

"Old Ekkthurian's lucky he doesn't have to look at

himself," whispered Charkky. "That frown would make a person sick to his stomach."

"He doesn't like having Red Unat up there," Mikk said. "He doesn't think it's seemly."

"He doesn't think anything's seemly," Charkky said. "Except making others miserable. I wish the hydrus would eat him."

"*Does* it eat folk?" Teb said, frowning.

They all stared at him. "Of course it does," Kkelpin said. "What else would it be wanting?"

"I don't know." But it seemed to Teb it wanted something else. He could still see in his mind the lure of those three terrifying faces. "I don't know what else it could want."

His songs had returned to him shortly after the hydrus attacked them. But there were new songs, too, come into his head then, ugly songs filled with a sense of the hydrus. And if it had put them there, why had it?

On the dais, Red Unat fluffed his feathers and shook his wings, then stood looking down at the mass of otters crowded into the cave. It was a moonlight meeting, and moonlight shone across his dark, mottled feathers, silhouetted against Thakkur's whiteness and against the pearly gleam of the mosaicked walls. The crowd of otters covered the floor of the cave in a great dark mass, and only the gleam of their eyes was clear. Though to the owl's sight, Teb thought, every detail of nose and whisker and claw would be visible. The owl spoke of the wars in the north, and it was not cheering news, for Quazelzeg was still moving south, slowly destroying everything in his path, food and shelter and herds.

"He has conquered the Seven Islands and enslaved the fishing villages of Thappan and destroyed the fishing boats—the hydrus did that in one raging night of terror. He has taken the mines at Neiwan. They are working women and children in the mines to make coal for Quazelzeg's forges and driving the men hitched to plows, instead of oxen. They ate the oxen and commandeered every horse and pack pony. They are raping the land, and already the conquered are starving. They will come down into Windthorst to deal with Ebis the Black soon enough. And," said the owl, turning to stare at the council, "once he has conquered the human world, he will prey on the animals in one way or another."

"But there is nothing here for him," said Ekkthurian. "Why would he want to come here?"

"He doesn't need a reason," said the owl. "He will invent a reason. Otter hides, maybe," he said, glaring at Ekkthurian. "Soft, warm otter hides for winter."

There was a great hush in the cave.

Charkky turned to look at Mikk, and their paws touched across Teb. Teb heard Jukka swallow as she pulled her heavy tail tighter around herself.

"And now the hydrus is returning, too," said the owl. "It is a more immediate threat. It moves south from Vaeal, along in the shallower coastal seas. There are three teams of little screech owls watching and tracking it, and they will warn the otters at Rushmarsh when it gets close and send a message to Ebis the Black."

"How can it be dangerous to Ebis the Black?" said Ekkthurian. "That hydrus can't go on land."

"It can move up the rivers to the inland ports, and it can destroy the lowland grain paddies during flooding cycle. It can move like a salamander over very little water when it wants to, on its great spread fins. And it will rend and kill anything that comes near the shore, reaching out with those long necks and wicked teeth. It is surely a slave of the dark," said the owl. "And it will kill for the dark."

Ekkthurian was quiet. The owl opened his beak in a soft clicking, as the hunter does before he swoops on his prey, and glared at Ekkthurian. Then Thakkur said softly, drawing attention to himself without ever raising his voice:

"Tebriel has brought us knives. They are effective against the hydrus. We must have more knives. And we must have swords and learn to use them."

Ekkthurian stared at Thakkur, his body going rigid with anger. Then he hissed through bared teeth, "You would not dare to arm this nation like humans! Such a thing is blasphemy!" He rose and stood staring out at the silent crowd of otters. "How would you acquire such weapons? Only by stealing! And that, too, Thak-

184

kur of Nightpool, is against all Ottra tradition!"

Thakkur spoke softly in the silent cave. His voice seemed to carry more clearly than Ekkthurian's. "I do not call it stealing," he said evenly, "if we take from the dark. I call it weakening the enemy."

There was a long moment of silence. Teb and Charkky exchanged a look. Then Ekkthurian barked, "What of the otters who must do such a deed? Do you not think many would be killed in a stealing raid? The owl is right, the dark raiders would skin any otter they could catch!"

"We are only a small band," cried Urikk. "We are not warriors, to be pitting ourselves against the dark forces."

"If the dark forces come here," said Thakkur, "we will have no choice. If they come in the form of the hydrus, and attack you in the sea, *you* will have no choice."

Ekkthurian and his friends were silent.

The owl began to fidget, grooming at a patch of tail feathers.

"Red Unat came here," Thakkur said, "to bring us news of the wars, not to listen to our bickering. I apologize for the entire council."

Teb thought Ekkthurian had been defeated, at least into temporary silence, but suddenly the thin otter rose again and stood at the edge of the dais with Urikk and Gorkk beside him, staring down at the gathered otters.

"*If* there is a dark," said Ekkthurian, "*if* the hydrus does return and attack us, you can lay the blame directly on the human boy, for it is *him* the hydrus comes seeking. *Him alone!* It never attacked any of us or came near Nightpool before the boy came here."

"If the boy leaves Nightpool," growled Gorkk, "the hydrus will follow him, and leave us unmolested."

Thakkur stood tall and still, an icy pillar staring at the three. "Would Nightpool deny sanction, deny safety and protection to the King of Auric?"

"What has the King of Auric to do with the boy?" Ekkthurian snapped. "We are speaking of a small, troublemaking boy."

"We are speaking of the King of Auric," said Thakkur. "Tebriel is the son of Everard of Auric, who was murdered by the dark forces. Tebriel is rightful heir to the throne."

"You are lying," shouted Ekkthurian. "He is only a homeless waif."

But the tide was turned, and the seated otters began to grumble at Ekkthurian. They knew Thakkur did not lie.

"Tebriel's memory has returned to him," said Thakkur. "He remembers his father's murder and his own enslavement at the hands of Sivich, of the dark."

"He *says* he's the king's son," said Ekkthurian. "Does that make it fact?"

"It does. And my visions show the same."

"And even if he were king," growled Ekkthurian,

186

"it would not change the harm he has brought to Night-pool. King or commoner, he must not be allowed to stay. He draws the hydrus here. He is a danger to us. He brings new ways that are a danger. The making of fire is insane; if fire is seen from the mainland, humans will be over here. The dark forces—if there are such—will surely be all over Nightpool, then. He is a danger, I tell you. A danger to all of us." Ekkthurian seemed to grow blacker in his rage. "And if the hydrus comes for him again, here, many of us could die in its jaws."

Teb stared across the heads of the gathered otters. Not one otter turned to look at him. He watched the three dark council members standing so fierce and still on the dais, and suddenly he had had enough. He was tight with fury as he stood up. All heads turned to look then.

"I am going," he said evenly. "I am going now. You can expect that by the time you leave this cave I will be away from Nightpool."

He walked out quietly, then ran the ledge to his cave, grabbed the knives and flint from the shelf, the cookpot, and shoved them into the pack, pulled Camery's diary from his tunic pocket and pushed it in, too, grabbed his flippers, and made his way in the moonlight around the stone rim of the island, and down the cliff to the little beach. The path of the moon lay white across the water. I will find Camery and Garit, he thought. And I will retake Auric. I should never have stayed at Nightpool once I got well and could walk. He knelt to pull on his flippers and was thankful he had them as he stared out at the black, moon-washed sea.

15

As he knelt to pull on his flippers, he heard Charkky shout, and Charkky and Mikk were plunging down the cliff. A crowd of otters streamed down after them, Jukka and Hokki and Litta and Kkelpin and dozens more. The owl soared overhead, and even Mitta climbed down, giving him such a soft, gentle look that it wrenched his heart.

"You can't go," Charkky said. "Thakkur . . ."

"I am going. It's time I went," Teb said coldly. And then the two otters were hugging him, fishy breath, stiff whiskers tickling him, and they weakened his resolve so, he had to push them away. "I have to," he said roughly. "I won't forget you. Not ever."

"But you can't go," Mikk said. "Thakkur told us . . ."

"I must. I am. I've had enough of Ekkthurian. I'm only causing trouble here. And . . ."

"And what?" said Mikk.

"And maybe Ekkthurian's right. Maybe I do draw the hydrus."

"That's what we're trying to tell you," Charkky interrupted. "Thakkur says if you do draw it, then you must stay."

Teb stared at him. "You're not making sense."

"Thakkur thinks that you—"

"That you would protect us best by staying," said the white otter, coming unseen from behind them. He gave Teb a level, loving look. But the kind of look that made Teb be still.

"If you do indeed draw the hydrus, Tebriel, then you must stay here with us. If you would help Nightpool at all, you will stay and draw the hydrus here."

Teb stared at Thakkur.

"The hydrus is of the dark, Tebriel. It will help to lay waste to all the coastal waters. Nightpool cannot stop Quazelzeg, but we might stop the hydrus. If it is drawn here, if it comes to seek us out . . ."

"To seek me out."

"Yes, to seek you out. You would be putting yourself in danger. But if you could lure it here, and we could kill it, you would not only help Nightpool, but you would also weaken the dark."

Teb looked for a long time at Thakkur. He thought about it; and he knew the white otter was right.

He shouldered his pack at last and picked up his fins and started back up the cliff toward the caves. Thakkur climbed beside him, and Charkky and Mikk, and all the otters followed.

Then at the crest he turned away from them, with a quiet word to Thakkur, and went to his cave alone.

He put away his possessions and stood looking out at the waves. Their white foam shone bright in the moonlight. He was very tired suddenly. He pulled off his tunic and lay down beneath Mitta's soft, warm blanket, clutching Camery's diary to him. Was he doing the right thing? Or should he be searching for Camery and leading the hydrus away from Nightpool?

He woke in the morning still clutching the little book and, hardly thinking, he opened it and began to flip through the pages. He found his name over and over, even in the last hasty messages. It did not appear, though, on the pages where the lines were shorter so they didn't fill the page. There was a rhythm to the length of these lines, and he began to study them.

He had printed out the words he had memorized in the great cave, "fox," "otter," "cape wolf," "owl," and "great cat," onto the back of Garit's message, with a sharp bit of charcoal. He looked at the words now. Yes, they were repeated several times in one of the short, rhythmic entries. It looked like—like his mother's Song of the Creatures. . . . He began to say the words, counting them off with his finger.

Yes, the names of the animals fell in the right places, all of them. He knew the song! He knew the words to this writing! Here was the key, to unlock the sounds and meanings of the strings of letters.

He sat down on his sleeping ledge, pulled the blanket around his legs, and began to study the song. Word for word he spoke it, studying the letters, seeing the sounds they made. Word for word he repeated the sounds, memorizing the shapes of the letters that made them. His stomach rumbled with hunger. Morning turned to noon, and the afternoon light settled to a golden depth before he stirred himself. He read the Song of the Creatures, and then, filled with excitement, and with fear that it might not work after all, he turned to another of the short, rhythmic entries. And he found he could read that, too, the Song of the Sacking of Perlayne. And he read another, and another. He was reading! The forms of all the letters made sounds for him now. He reread every song. He knew them all, of course, and the sense of power it gave him to be recognizing their words, written down, was wonderful. And then at last, afraid to try but knowing he must, knowing he *could*, he began to read the words he did not know by heart. He started to read the other entries in Camery's diary, beginning with the last, urgent passages. His efforts were slow and halting, as he sounded out the words, but the messages were clear.

Sivich came to the tower this morning to look me over, the way a horse trader looks at a colt. I don't like it. If he takes me from this place, I will leave the diary for you, Teb. It's all we have left of being together, and maybe you will find it.

The palace has been silent all day. They rode out for the coast at dawn, heavily armed. I am feeling very lonely. If I had a weapon I would go down among the jackals and try to get out. And die there if I failed, and maybe be happier. What is the good of staying in this tower and growing old and dying here and never living at all?

I feel better today. If he takes me out of here, no matter what he does to me, it will be better than the tower.

Something is happening in the courtyard. It is night, the servants are asleep. I can hardly see to write. There is some kind of movement down there, but the jackals are not growling.

And then the last lines, hastily written:

Someone has opened the door at the base of the tower, someone is coming up. I love you, Teb.
It's all right, Teb. I'm going away, but I won't write any name. I love you.

He sat for a long time, staring out at the brightening sea. Otters appeared, cascading off the cliff down by Thakkur's, but he did not join them.

Surely it was Garit who had taken her away. If it had been Sivich, she wouldn't have had time to write those last words after he appeared at the top of the stair. Besides, that entry had been written in the tower, and the owl had found the diary in the brewer's house at Bleven.

She had carried it with her. But she hadn't written in it anymore.

He put the little book on the shelf, and took down Garit's crumpled note. And now he read it easily:

Do you give Tebriel into the care of the Graven Light and make him safe and teach him until the lion gathers its brood and the dove comes from the cage like an eagle. And until the dragon screams.

He sat thinking about the message. Surely Garit was the lion; it was an old family joke that he could be as fierce and as kind as the great speaking cats of the north, and his beard was as red as theirs. And the lion's brood would be the army Garit had promised Teb, to win back Auric. And surely the dove was Camery. *Had* she come from her cage like an eagle? To fight beside Garit, perhaps?

"And until the dragon screams," Teb thought. Those words gave him goose bumps, and he sat frowning and puzzled, almost grasping something, feeling a rising elation and a power within himself that was heady and frightening. And impossible. *Until the dragon screams . . . Until the dragon sings*, he thought. *Until I sing* . . . He felt the strength within himself and did not know what to make of it.

Across the sea the bright gold sky was drowning in a heavy layer of mountainous cloud, and the sea had turned leaden and looked cold. The crowd of otters swimming out there didn't seem to mind; they floated on their backs laughing and eating sea urchins.

Would the hydrus return to Nightpool? *Was* it looking for him?

Why?

What might it want with him? Did it have to do with this power he felt? With the impossible wonder he felt? The dark wanted him. . . . Because he touched a power he could not understand?

Who am I? What am I? He felt as uncertain, as lost to his own true identity, as he had felt when he had had no memory at all.

He put on his fins at last, sighted the deep, calmer pool below, and dove far out and straight and swam with strong strokes out toward the feeding otters. He sped along and was strong enough now with the flippers' power to outmaneuver the waves. His flippers were like an otter's webbed feet, driving him through the sea.

He doesn't even have webs between his toes, Litta

had said once, laughing. He looked back toward the cliff to see a line of sentries standing watch for the sea hydrus, and he thought Thakkur was right, stolen weapons would be a comfort when the creature came.

He reached the feeding otters, and Mikk started a game of catch with a small sea urchin. Later he gave Teb a lesson in diving and holding his breath, and Teb was pleased that he was growing more skilled. He had managed to pry three abalones loose and was taking them home to his cave to cook when Thakkur sent for him. He dropped the abalone on his sleeping shelf, slipped on his leather tunic, though it was very tight for him now, and went along to Thakkur's cave.

The owl was there, and soon Charkky and Mikk and a good many others, too, came to join them, to plan a stealing raid for weapons to use against the hydrus.

"Sivich's men are rounding up stray horses on the meadows," the owl said. "If they camp on the eastern meadows near Nightpool, I will come to alert you. You can slip weapons away in the darkness, move off quickly again to the sea."

"There is an underwater cave at the mainland, near our south shore," Thakkur said. "We can hide the weapons there, hide ourselves there if need be."

"But not you, of course," said the owl. "Your white coat would show far too brightly; and Nightpool cannot risk losing its leader."

"I mean to cover my coat with mud," said Thakkur.

"Do you think I would send otters into a danger I won't face?"

"We will vote on it in council," said Shekken. "We do not want to risk losing you."

"You will not vote in council. This is my decision, not Nightpool's."

But it was not to come so quickly, this stealing of weapons. Sivich called in his troops to make a series of raids north of Branthen, where attacks by the growing underground had fouled Quazelzeg's plans, and no more soldiers were seen gathering horses until late in the fall as the sea took on an early phosphorescent gleam like fires under the water. Then the phosphorescence washed away and the water turned chill and gray, and the owl came winging down over Nightpool on a blustery afternoon to say that a band of Sivich's men was working toward the coast, gathering strays. He went back to watch them, circling so high he was only a speck, and returned at dusk to report they had camped conveniently close to the south cliffs that fell down to the sea.

The moon was at half, and still too bright, but the wind was so high that it would hide any sound of their approach. They were a band of nine as they slipped down the south cliff and into the sea, Charkky and Mikk and Teb, Kkelpin and Jukka and Hokki, Thakkur and Shekken and Berthekk. And the owl, of course, circling overhead silent and invisible. Teb carried one knife in the pocket of his breechcloth. Thakkur carried the other. Berthekk carried a coil of twine Mitta had braided for them, to secure the weapons to logs, to drag them home. The only thing that could be seen clearly during that swim was Thakkur's white head, and the paler oval of Teb's own face. The moment they came up out of the water at the foot of the mainland cliff, Thakkur found a patch of mud and smeared himself with it, and Teb did the same, covering all his bare skin, until soon the two of them looked little different from the others. Except that Teb was a good deal taller.

They climbed the cliff in silence, and as they came out onto the grassy plain they could smell the horses, a hearty, sweet smell that stirred a powerful longing in Teb. They could see the camp in the distance, where the campfire still smoldered. It was late, and they hoped the camp was asleep, hoped the shadows passing back and forth in front of the red embers were only the legs of grazing horses. The little band crept forward as the owl circled overhead in the heaving wind. The horses would be nervous, restless in the wind, ready to run if Teb could free them. That would cripple their pursuers and be a setback for Sivich. A very small thing, in this war. But he supposed every small thing counted for something.

As they drew near, the horses began to stir. Teb heard one snort and knew they were watching the dark shadows creeping toward them. He tensed to run, or to fight. He could see the way the horses moved that they were tied to a common tether rope, each on its own short rope that he would have to jerk free.

As he fumbled at ropes, whispering gently to the horses, loosing one and calming it, then loosing the next, he could see the dark shapes of the otters moving among the sleeping men, see the occasional glint of a steel blade as they confiscated weapons. A soldier snorted and turned over, and everyone froze. Several of the men snored. A soldier moaned, and Teb saw an otter back away. He had loosed one line of horses and begun on the other, the first animals moving off softly into the night. They had likely been loose on the pastures a long time; they wouldn't linger here. Near to him a sleeping man rolled over, sighing. There was the tiny clink of metal against metal as someone worked too hastily. But the wind hid many mistakes. The horses stirred as he loosed the last of them. Then the owl came swooping and one horse bolted, then another. "Run," someone whispered. "They're waking. . . ." The horses wheeled and went galloping off, and even the wind couldn't hide that thunder. Teb and the otters fled, the otters clanking now with their burden of weapons. Teb grabbed a handful from someone, another, until he, too, was loaded down. There was a shout behind them, some swearing, sounds of confusion, and then of running feet, too close. . . .

But there was the cliff, and they plunged over its

side, tossing the weapons down to the sand, grabbing at the stone as they climbed and slid down; and they grabbed up weapons again from the sand and dove into the waves and down, and it was very easy to dive, to sink, so loaded with heavy weapons.

They came up inside the cave, Teb flanked and guided on both sides by swimming bodies. He sucked in air. He could see Thakkur now, a pale smear among invisible swimmers. He kicked hard to keep afloat, with the burden of the weapons. Then someone was pushing him toward the cave wall, and he clung there with one hand, clutching the weapons with the other.

16

They stayed in the cave until the moon had set, then headed home through the black water, pulling the weapons behind them tied to driftwood logs scavenged from the beach. They had captured thirteen spears, eleven swords, and five good knives, as well as four good bows and two quivers full of arrows. They took the weapons to Thakkur's cave, cleaned and dried them with moss, and polished the blades with fish oil to keep rust from starting, after their salty bath in the sea. Then they all slept the day around and ended with a big meal at sunset. Teb laid his fire in a niche in the rock above his cave and brought a pot full of steamed clams to the feast in Thakkur's cave, where Thakkur hefted a sword and thrust with it, looking very pleased.

"We will form teams of soldiers and train with the

weapons until we are skilled both in the sea and from the cliffside." His dark eyes shone with purpose. "And perhaps, in our own way, we will help against the dark."

For days afterward, otters crowded in to look at the weapons, hahing at their gleam and sharpness, and there was more than one cut paw from careless enthusiasm. Ekkthurian came and looked, and went away silent, and it would not be until the hydrus returned, hunting for Tebriel, that the dark otter would speak out again with his usual venom. Something seemed to go out of Ekkthurian after the stealing of the weapons, something to lay a hand on his vile manner and silence him. He sulked around Nightpool with Urikk and Gorkk, and the three otters fished alone, north up the coast toward Rushmarsh. Sometimes Ekkthurian was not seen for days, as if he slept the time away in his cave out of boredom and anger, perhaps. Early winter brought the runs of silverheads and squarefins. And schools of migrating seals and whales passed beyond Nightpool, and the sea was brilliant again at night with hidden flame from millions of tiny phosphorescent creatures. Teb practiced his swimming and diving, and holding his breath for longer times. When the water grew too cold to stay in long, he practiced with sword and spear, and when storms blew he sat in his cave, or with Mitta or Charkky and Mikk, weaving sometimes, for they always needed string bags. He ripped out the seams of his leather tunic, which had grown too small, and laced them with a two-inch gap, with strands cut from a bridle rein. And he made new flippers for swimming, for he had well outgrown the first pair.

In these quiet times, he tried to delve deeper into the dreams that came at night, and into the sense of growing power that was with him now, heady and mysterious. What power? What did it mean? *Was* it linked somehow to the dragon? Or did he only imagine that? The power he felt was not of the body, but of the mind. Or, perhaps, of soul. Part of a magical force that, he thought, could be made to grow, could be used with astonishing wonder—if only he understood it. If only he had the courage to learn its source. And yet he could not truly believe what he guessed at. What was he? Who was he? What secrets had his parents never told him?

Winter seemed incredibly long and severe, and twice the island was covered with snow, a rare treat. The otters spent days sliding down the snowy inner cliffs and never seemed to tire of the sport. Their heavy tails made fine sleds, and Teb found a driftwood board for himself and put away all other thoughts for the joy of days of sledding.

But gales blew, too. And at last everyone moved into the center of the island again. The otters' diet, in winter, ran heavier to eels, which could be dug along the shore where they had burrowed, and Teb learned to tolerate them roasted. Then the coming of spring brought fresh shellfish again and a more varied menu. Teb took to the sea with the rest, eagerly pulling on his flippers and leaping in to fish and play complicated games of skill. He learned to dive deeper, thrusting down with the power of the fins. "It's all in knowing how," Mikk said. "Small breath held in, then larger, then larger, before ever you dive. Until the last breath goes down into stretched lungs. And then hold that one as you drop down. Let out a few bubbles at a time until you feel comfortable—you'll know when to come up, all right." A diving rock helped, too, to weight Teb for deep dives, and he could drop it before buoying to the surface. He had built a new raft to put the rocks on, and the swords, and a collecting bag.

He could not see as well underwater as the otters, or stay under as long, and he was constantly shaking the water out of his ears. They never did; their ears closed when they dove, just as did their noses. Teb examined Charkky's ear to see how, and found a little flap of furred skin that drew closed when the water pressed over it. He was growing so tall he had to bend over to look, and that seemed very strange. All the otters seemed shorter now, and it made him uncomfortable to be taller than Thakkur, because he thought of Thakkur as tall. The old otter looked tall when he stood among the others. Thakkur *held* himself tall.

"You are growing into a young man, Tebriel. Many human soldiers go into battle no older than you."

"Do you see me in battle, when you look in the clamshell?"

"Sometimes. But the visions are vague and uncertain."

"What else do you see? I feel . . . I feel there are things about myself that are still hidden. As if my memory has not all returned."

"Or as if, perhaps, those certain things were never known to you?"

"Perhaps," Teb said. "What is it you see in the shell?"

"I see the hydrus returning, Tebriel. I think perhaps my plan was not a wise one—to use you as bait."

"If it wants me, if the dark wants me, it will find me anywhere. Only, why does it? What am I, that the dark would want me?"

Thakkur paced, staring out at the sunstruck sea. The water was calm and deep blue under the warm spring sky. A flock of gulls wheeled close to the cave, then was gone. Out in the sea along the underwater shelf, a group of otters was fishing, banking and twisting to snatch at a flashing school of silver sprats, the otters more playful than hungry. Thakkur stopped pacing and faced Teb, his back to the open sky, his white whiskered face in shadow.

"You were alone with the hydrus in my vision, and I felt a cold fear for you. And I felt a sense of power grown great, Tebriel, under some terrible stress. Only, I could not tell whose power—yours, or the hydrus's."

205

Teb sat very still.

Thakkur began to pace again, his paws held still before him, his broad tail describing a white moon each time he turned, his dark eyes troubled.

"This time, Tebriel, the vision brings no certainty. This time I think you must follow your own instinct. You must leave Nightpool or you must stay, according to what your deepest inner self tells you." Thakkur looked at him, frowning. "There is more here, of power and of meaning, than my poor visions can sort out."

"There is something you are not telling me."

Thakkur did not answer.

"Why not? It isn't fair. If you know . . ."

Silence. They looked at each other for a long time, Thakkur's gaze veiled and secretive, yet very direct, as if he held back only because he must. As if perhaps this was something Teb must unravel for himself, without being told—without help from anyone.

"Because I must discover for myself?"

The white otter nodded.

Teb turned to stare out at the sea. He wanted to say what he guessed. And yet he was afraid to say it. One thing was certain, though. He would stay at Nightpool until the hydrus returned. No inner fear, no deliberation, could make him turn away now from facing it. For in some way, the hydrus was a part of the power he felt.

Was it a power that could turn to evil as well as good? Was the hydrus a part of that evil? He knew he was drawn to it, to a confrontation impossible to avoid. The hydrus could make him lose a part of himself, and so he must destroy it.

But it would be another year, nearly to the day he spoke with Thakkur of the visions, before they met, and the hydrus had swum a long way and wreaked great damage along the coasts of countless continents. Nightpool knew of the wars from the owl, and that Sivich had settled in well, in the three nations of Branthen just north of Windthorst. They knew that in the more northerly countries, other of Quazelzeg's captains held strong power. If there was a resistance, it did little more than frustrate Quazelzeg, and there was no change of rule. Perhaps the heterhuman folk of the far lands on the other side of Tirror, and pocketed in colonies on the near continents, were moving in some kind of secret resistance. There was no way to know, for they were secretive and mingled little, in these modern times, with human or animal folk.

The little owls came first and cried to beware, that the hydrus was near. Then they went away, content with their warning, lifting and tilting on the wind in close flight, screaming their hunting cry. Then the hydrus was sensed by vibration far out in the sea as a band of otters chased silver sea trout along the edge of the sunken continent.

Thakkur appointed a double watch, two armed bands always on duty, and the weapons were kept oiled and sharp. The first time the hydrus came, it raged in from the outer deeps, driving hard at a band of fishing otters, diving when they dove, terrifying them until an armed band joined them, sweeping out to surround the great beast.

They bloodied it and slashed its sides and tore a wound down one head. They could see the pale, healed scars where its throat had been cut before, and its eye injured. They had grown skilled indeed with the heavy weapons, thrusting and slashing in the water until it backed and fled.

The second attack, four weeks later, brought it rising suddenly from the shallow landward bay, where it had come in deep and quietly in the night. It thrust up at the black sheltering rim of the island so the rock shuddered and the caves echoed. The defending otters leaped down onto it from the cliff and bloodied its gaping, reaching faces before it was driven back. One strong young male, Perkketh, clung to its neck and thrust at its head with his sword while others cut deep gashes in its leathery hide. But it killed Perkketh with one thrusting flip of its head as it heaved him against the cliff.

The Ottra nation mourned Perkketh and made ceremony for him in the meeting cave and buried him in the cave of burial close beside the green marsh. They planted his grave with starflowers. And in his farewell prayer for Perkketh, Thakkur said words that set Teb to thinking in a new way.

"Not of the sea and not of the land, the Ottra are

wanderers all in that thin world that lies between. Each to its own place must cling, even in death must cling. And what comes after death when we rise anew, only a wisdom far greater than our wisdom can ordain. The Graven Light take Perkketh now and keep him in joy and in dignity."

The third attack by the hydrus was close to the north shore of Nightpool just at Shark Rock, as Teb and Charkky were coming up at dusk from gathering oysters. It was low tide, and the oyster beds were exposed far out into the sea. Teb could see Ekkthurian and his two companions moving along at the far outer edge of the oyster beds just beside the sea trench, dragging a string bag of oysters between them. When the hydrus came up suddenly from the trench, Urikk dropped the bag and ran, but it snapped up Ekkthurian and Gorkk, then charged Teb and Charkky and Mikk as the guarding band on the cliff swarmed down. Teb crouched, his knife ready. The hydrus shook the two otters it held, bellowing, and reached with its third head for Teb. Teb dodged and leaped away, slashing at the reaching face, and blood spurted. The hydrus dropped Ekkthurian, screaming, then dropped Gorkk. The otter lay writhing and snarling. The hydrus advanced on Teb, all its attention on him, holding him frozen with the stare of those six immense eyes; yet it did not reach for him, and knowledge filled him, in that moment, that it did not want him dead.

When it did reach, it was gently, the middle head

thrusting out, and its great thick lips mumbled over his face so he wanted to retch. He could not move. He knew it would carry him away, and his fear was so terrible it would be almost a relief to have it over with; then suddenly it lurched away as the otters attacked, thrusting and slashing: the otter guards from the cliff battled it back toward the sea. Teb was fighting beside them now. Otters leaped to its neck, and Teb leaped; they attacked the three heads until it bellowed with rage and twisted, flinging them off, and thrashed back into the deep sea. They stood looking after it, panting.

"Did we kill it?" Charkky said at last.

"I don't know," Teb said. "We hurt it, though. I think we hurt it badly."

Several otters were being helped up the cliff trailing blood, Ekkthurian and Gorkk among them. Teb could see Mitta hurrying along the high ledge, with half a dozen others, to tend the wounded. He stared out at the sea where the waters still showed pink, then turned away from the group of otter warriors.

He walked for a long time along the edge of the water, rounding the island but seeing, in his mind, the wounded otters. Seeing Perkketh dead.

These things should never have happened. They must not happen again. He knew, now, that he must go away. That this one time, Thakkur was wrong. He must lead the hydrus, not here to the island again, but away from it. When he had circled the island, and come to where otters were gathered outside Thakkur's cave, he learned there had been two deaths more. Gorkk, and a strapping otter named Tekket, who left behind him a wife and four cubs. Teb went to Thakkur, then, and found him alone. He sat in the cave in silence as the white otter puttered about, his paws busy for the first time Teb could remember. When at last he turned, Teb could see his grief.

"I am going away," Teb said. "I will lead the hydrus away."

"No. We will kill the hydrus, Tebriel. Given time, we can. If you go now, every otter will feel that he has failed, will know that you led it away because we have failed to kill it."

"I will say that I go to search for my sister. That is true. And I feel—I would search for the dragon, Thakkur. The singing dragon."

Thakkur nodded, and again there was a long silence between them, as understanding grew. Then he said softly, "Yes. But first you mean to seek the hydrus."

"I must."

Thakkur turned away, to stare out at the sea. When he faced Teb again, the sadness robed him heavily. He studied Teb; and saw in Teb's face the resolve that would not be swayed. He said at last, "Give us, then, this night for ceremony, Tebriel. A feast of good-bye. Such a gathering would ease the pain of leave-taking for all of us. Will you allow us that?"

And so there was a feast, and gift giving, and Thakkur's quiet predictions beforehand, which now came so clearly in the clamshell, as if Teb's own increased power helped to bring them. For Teb *did* feel a power that excited him with its promise. And when, late in the evening, he sang the Song of the Creatures, he held the gathered otters silent and transfixed as he spun out living scenes of the speaking animals, amazing himself as well as them with the power of his conjuring. He felt his strength surging, felt forces within himself that he could not put shape to, felt skills begin to rise, filled with wonder and power. For long moments after the song was finished, the otters sat in awe; it was Ekkthurian who broke the stillness by rising to stomp away. Teb hardly noticed, for the sense of promise that filled him. Promise of a wonder he could not even name. A wonder that, now, gave added meaning to Thakkur's predictions, which the old otter had spoken quietly while they sat alone.

"You will ride the winds of Tirror, Tebriel. And you will touch humankind and change it. You will see more than any creature or human sees, save those of your own special kind.

"I see mountains far to the north, and you will go there among wonderful creatures and speak to them, and know them."

Thakkur predicted threat as well as wonder. "I see a street in Sharden's city narrow and mean. There is danger there and it reeks of pain. Take care, Tebriel, when you journey into Sharden."

The ceremony had made bright new songs tumble

into Teb's head, verses that captured, for all time, those moments of pleasure as the otters presented him with gold and pearls and polished shells and corals, verses that would bring their voices back years hence, and their gentle, bright expressions and funny grins.

There was feasting, the special lighted torches Charkky and Mikk had made, the great fire to roast the fish and shellfish in his honor. They laughed, and played the otter games of three-shell and clap, and it was late indeed when all found their ways to cave and bed. Teb lay on his stone shelf staring out at the stars and hearing the sea. He did not sleep.

He rose at first light and dove far out and swam for a long time in the cold sea, trying to lose the terrible homesickness that gripped him. Trying to lose the fear with which he began this journey to confront the hydrus; trying to understand better the sense of power that was now a part of himself, to understand how to deal with it. When he returned to his cave, there was Thakkur, coming to say a private good-bye.

"You will return, I have no doubt of it." The white otter's eyes were as deep and fathomless as the sea itself. "Go in joy, Tebriel. Go with the blessing of The Maker. Go in the care of the Graven Light."

Teb took up his pack at last and lashed it to his waist. He gave Thakkur a long, steady look, then stepped to the edge of the cliff and dove far out and deep, cutting the water cleanly and striking out at once against the incoming swells. As quickly as that he left

Nightpool, and his tears mixed with the salty sea. As quickly as that he settled all his own past behind him, all his years on Nightpool, as one would settle a cape around his shoulders like a strong protection. He faced ahead into the unknown and the fearsome, letting the challenge touch him and draw him on.

17

Teb remained on the meadows above the sea cliff only long enough to feel out of place and exposed. The band of horses he had startled as he climbed the cliff had disappeared beyond the hills. No one was in sight, but soldiers could appear from the hills; it was foolish to be traveling so openly across this land in the daytime. Even when he kept to the small stands of woods and the low valleys, he felt exposed. When he had passed the point of Jade Beach, he made his way down the cliff and walked along the rocks beside the sea, where he was safer from humans.

In midafternoon he gathered clams and mussels, built a small fire, and made a meal. He passed the cave of the ghost, and stopped to stare in as the hundreds of birds swept screaming on their own wind low above his head. The rocks were slippery as he crossed past the cave. He kept watching the sea, foolishly, for the sight of familiar otter faces and knew he would see none. He camped well before dark, away from the edge of the cliff, in a small stand of almond trees that grew nestled between two hills. He could hear the sea's pounding close by, and the smell of the salt wind was comfortable, but he was too far from the edge of the cliff to be reached by those three giant heads, if the hydrus should come in the night. He felt it would come; he felt a sense of it almost as if he could smell it.

Maybe he only imagined that it wanted him. Maybe he only imagined the power he thought he could touch and that it seemed to want. Why would *he* have some mysterious power? Maybe he was just a homeless boy trying to become a man by imagining powers that did not exist.

But the songs had power. He had felt that power touch him, from his mother's songs. And he had seen his own songs touch the otters. The power of the songs, he thought . . .

And he slept.

The hydrus was there when he woke. He didn't know it was. He yawned and stretched and went down to the sea to wash, as he had done every day for four years, hardly looking, wanting that salty bath.

He swam, staying in close in a shallow bay, watching the sea now, wishing he could feel vibrations as the

otters did; but feeling certain, too, that this new power he felt within himself would tell him if the hydrus was close. He came out and, as he dried in the early-rising sun, gathered his breakfast from the rocks.

Behind him the sea lapped gently. The early sun was warm on his back, its light reflected in flashes of his blade as he pried the mussels loose. The young ones were the most tender. He heard the cry of a passing gull; then suddenly the hydrus was over him, snatching him up, its teeth across his middle, his feet inside its mouth, his arms pinioned. All he could see was lips and face, those huge muddy eyes, and the land receding fast. And each time he moved, it bit tighter. His fist was clamped on his knife, but its teeth pressed on his arm. And though the hydrus said no word, he felt that it would speak. He hung rigid in its mouth watching the waves crest before its swimming feet. Then the other two heads came around to look at him, and the four muddy eyes saw everything about him. He didn't want to look anymore, yet couldn't help but look, and he felt his mind go empty. He was so afraid that at last terror left him, and he fell into a cold, emotionless state, where every detail was magnified. He watched its black, finned feet breaking the water. He watched the sea flash below. He studied the black pitted skin of its body, torn with bleeding wounds, and he smelled the creature's blood. He saw every detail of the two faces, the elongated muzzles and wide mouths, the pale skin of the faces contrasted with the black wrinkled hide of the body, the coarse, bristling hair and muddy eyes: human faces warped into terrible parodies.

It traveled for a long way out into the sea. Teb lost track of time, but the sun came up high overhead and burned him, and then dropped behind the hydrus as the creature swept on. There was no hint of land, not even a jutting rock. The sea was the dark color that speaks of terrible depths. Fish swerved away from its swimming wake, fish that live only in the vast open sea. The sun dropped low in the sky on the watery horizon behind them. And then at last and suddenly, the hydrus dove; Teb gulped air once, then water closed over him and the hydrus was speeding down and down through water as dark as night. He would die now. Why was it diving? Why didn't it just crush him in its jaws? Down and down in the darkness—or had it begun to rise again? It didn't matter—he was drowning; his ears rang and his lungs were tight; he had to breathe in water, couldn't hold any longer.

The hydrus broke out of water into a pocket of air; Teb gulped breath, panting. And then it dropped him back into the water; and as he floundered, he saw that stone walls surrounded the pool of sea where he struggled to keep afloat. He stared up at the stone walls and at a small smear of sky far above. Was he at the bottom of an immense stone chimney, somehow flooded by the sea? Or in a flooded tower perhaps? The hydrus was gone. Turning, he discovered the opening through which it had vanished, and saw the huge slab of stone blocking it, the water still rocking where the hydrus had pulled the rock across. His fear made him panic; he thrashed uselessly in the rolling water and gulped a mouthful and choked. He tried to calm himself, then began to study the rock wall, searching for handholds, for a way to climb.

Teb's capture did not go unheeded. In Nightpool, Thakkur was shocked awake from a short nap, sat up in his cave confused, then, gathering his mind into clarity, went immediately to the big meeting cave, to the sacred shell. He stood letting the smoky surface dim and glow as he repeated and repeated Teb's name; and Thakkur saw, and watched for a long time that terrible swimming voyage with Teb grasped in the mouth of the hydrus; but the visions faded and vanished before ever the hydrus dove.

Others knew of Teb's capture, too. Though not so soon as Thakkur knew. At first Dawncloud knew only that something dark came seeking into her mind, wanting the songs she sang, something that coupled with her thoughts and tried to suck the words from her and distort them. As Thakkur strained to retain the dim vision in the foggy depths of the clamshell, as he saw at last the figure of Tebriel trapped among drowned stone, Dawncloud keened in bewilderment, then rocked in growing anger on her nest. The five dragonlings hissed with fury and stared north, and Seastrider rose up on the edge of the nest and keened out in fire-breathing confusion, knowing something was wrong but not able to understand what.

In the drowned, ruined tower of the castle Braudel, of the drowned city of Cophillon of the great drowned continent of Ancotas, a very long way from Nightpool, Tebriel at last found footholds sufficient to climb the height of the stone wall. It wasn't easy climbing, for the mason had set the stones as tightly and evenly as he knew how, and only where a bit of mortar had washed away by high seas could Teb find any foothold. Seven times he climbed partway, then fell back, until it grew too dark to try. The night seemed endless as he hung in the chill, dark water clinging to one small niche in the stone, kicking to keep afloat and terrified he would fall asleep and lose his grip on the stone and drown. He began again to climb at first light. The hydrus had not returned, but he could hear it some-times thrashing and heaving outside the wall. He thought of its wounds and hoped it was dying. He climbed again and again, weaker now, and his thirst was terrible. And then at last, bleeding and clutching, he gained the top of the wall and lay along it, panting and shivering, then fell into a druglike doze, waking sometimes to hear the sea pound below and to lie lis-tening helplessly for the hydrus's return. He hadn't the strength or the courage to drop over the outside of the wall into the heaving sea. His head swam with blackness, and soon he was sweating and burning with the sun's heat. He didn't see until much later, when he woke fully, the three cupped niches along the wall's top, where stones had broken away. They were filled with rainwater, and when he did see, he edged along the wall to them and drank them dry, unwilling to leave any for later. Who knew what would happen later?

He could not see land in any direction and could not imagine how far from Auric he might be. The sea heaved and rolled in a different way out here so far from land, its flowing surface broken only by the cluster of emerging tile rooftops and stone walls, ragged and crusted with barnacles, that thrust up out of the water. He knew he was seeing just the highest towers and tallest buildings of the drowned city. The exposed windows of the topmost rooms had lost their shutters, and looked hollow and forlorn. The walls below the surface went all wavy with the movement of the sea. The water all around the sunken city was lighter, greener, marking the shallowness of this place. It must have been a mountaintop city. The sea turned dark a way off, as the shelf dropped into the awesome depths, as Charkky called the deepest sea.

Which way was Auric? The sun sat so perfectly overhead that he had no idea of direction. Later, when the sun dropped, he would know. He could jump then, and swim for it. If he rested in the water, took his time, he could swim for hours.

If nothing bothered him. When night came he would

follow the stars of the nine sisters, and Mimmilette, which Thakkur called the one-legged cub, and the pale smear of Casscassonne, Tirror's false moon.

He leaned down to stare at the outside of the wall, then began to pry off barnacles and stuff the tough shellfish into his mouth. He hung there eating until he began to feel sick, then righted himself and sat astraddle again. The outside of the wall was rougher and would be easy to climb down. He was squinting around at the horizon, trying to see a smudge of land, when a stirring below made him turn back to stare down inside the tower. The hydrus was slipping through into it, huddling its three heads down to clear the space, then churning and flapping in the water as if it sought his drowned body. Then it stilled and stared up at him with all three faces. And it was now at last that the hydrus spoke to him, filling him with fear and disgust. One head spoke, and then another, echoing back and forth, the voices harsh and resonant and pounding in his mind, pounding all through him so he went weak and sweating. And it was then he knew deep inside himself that he could not escape. That it would have him, that if he climbed outward into the sea it would be out there at him in seconds, that somehow it would have him down from the tower. Every word it spoke increased his fear, though afterward he could not remember those words, only knew their meaning. It would have his mind; it would own him. The creature's mind pulled at him so he felt he was falling down into the dark circle of the sea beside it. . . .

He did not fall. His mind went dizzy and empty, and he lay unconscious along the top of the wall unaware of anything, unaware of the hydrus that tried to command him. He was aware only of a world within, of songs exploding to show scenes of battle, ballads intricate and vivid with the seething life of Tirror.

The song gave him ships headed through heaving seas for a forested coast; it cried out in cadences that made men and horses leap into the sea and swim through surf to drive back defending armies; the song showed the land fallen waste, the crops and towns burned. It showed new cities rising slowly amid fear and starvation as the conquerers worked their slaves.

Then he saw children gathered, singing the same song he heard, and he saw the bard who led them, standing tall between the feet of a pearl-white dragon who sang with him; he heard her song so clearly he started. And she made the songs come to life more clearly than he ever had. He could hear the shouts, and smell the horses and the blood, smell the sweat of the soldiers and hear their cries. The dragon made it more real than ever he could have done. And he knew her—for it was himself there standing between her claws. He was certain all at once what his sense of power meant, and knew why he longed for the dragon: He knew at last with thundering clarity what he was born to do. The word "dragonbard" flared in his mind, and all the songs he knew glowed bright and waiting, meant to be told, meant to be sung, coupled with the voice of the dragon. It was bard and dragon together who made the songs live, made them real in the listener's mind as if he were truly there hearing the shouting and feeling the pain and joy. She was a time-creature, taking the listener back, making him live that time so he knew it as a part of himself. Dragon and bard together, the making of song, the making of a magical reliving, the continued rebirth of life, and of hope.

But then the brightness faded and his songs began to darken and to change, and he could not prevent the changing. Now he saw himself *forcing* the will of the dragon, making it sing new, dark words. And in the darkness, he knew that dragons had no right to make songs, that only he could make them, painted in darkness, and that the dragon must be made to follow him. Oh, yes, she would follow. The colors of *his* songs were dark and fine, and a great crowd gathered to hear him and to believe him. He felt his own power rising, growing, saw the throngs that mobbed around him, yearning for his words. Yes, this was the way, the way of the dark, the way the hydrus showed him, yes. This was what he would do with his life—bring the dragon to him and train her to sing as *he* wished, as the dark wished, for he was the master, not she. His vision was steeped in shadows and black mists that matched the voice in his mind, strong and soothing and shaping his need, pushing back the flare of conscience that prickled him.

He lay, at last, spent, spread-eagled along the wall. The circle of sea at the bottom of the stone tower was empty now. Above him the sky was dark but cloud-driven, the sun long since gone and the sea wind chilled. He lay there for hours, listening, seeing, changing inside himself. He thought of the hydrus now with warmth and knew it had been right to bring him here, knew it was the wisest of creatures, knew it would care for him.

He sat up, ignoring thirst. He ate some barnacles, sucking their meager juice. He must bring the dragon here, the small dragon, the one called Seastrider, yes, and together they would make their songs here. He would train her here under the knowing guidance of the hydrus, he would train her to the true way. Dark songs, yes, compelling songs to lead in righteousness the hordes that must be led. . . .

At last he slept, flung across the wall.

18

How long the hydrus kept Teb he had no idea. Time swam in dark patches of dream, and in between he drank from the collected dew in the niches, and ate barnacles, and slept, or thought he did these things. He was sure of nothing but the thoughts of the hydrus guiding him as he huddled atop the stone wall, chill at night and burning in the daytime, calling and calling to the dragon, demanding that she come to him.

But then, sometimes his mind would lock against the hydrus in weak battle and he would lie shivering, knowing something that he could not bring clear, and then he did not call out to the young dragon, but weakly warned her away. Yet these transgressions were short-lived, and then he would once more cleave to the dark will of the hydrus, knowing that this was the true way.

He hardly remembered any life before this. The otters were a vague memory of something imagined, and there was nothing before that at all. Only the demands of the hydrus were real. The dragon must come; it was urgent that she come so they could begin their quest.

Oh, he would be a persuasive singer—the hydrus told him so. His voice was clear and strong, very right for the ballads, and the visions he made were sharp with detail. Linked with the dragon the songs would be rich beyond belief, and soon Tirror would know the real tales, and Quazelzeg would bring to all the nations a time of truth and new rule. For only in Quazelzeg's plan *was* there truth. Only when all humankind and animals served the true masters in unquestioning obedience, putting aside their own unorganized and arbitrary pursuits, swearing fealty only to Quazelzeg's vision, would there be true design and harmony on Tirror. And wouldn't he sing of Quazelzeg's virtues? All the songs, now, were filled with his virtues. Teb's commitment built, and the small voice inside that cried out against the hydrus's deceit was stilled by Teb himself.

Yet that voice would not be completely stilled and made him twist and fight in his sleep. But then when he woke, the dark would take him once more and he would call out to the dragon with all the lure he knew. She must come, the one dragon must come to him for him to be whole and skilled and able at Quazelzeg's work. He must teach the joys of obedience, show each commoner the true way in serving the benevolent dark masters. And it was through the power of the dragon songs, bringing alive such joys, that all commoners could be made to understand.

He had no notion how much time had passed, nor did he care, the morning the hydrus brought him down off the wall simply by commanding him to dive. He dove willingly down into the small circle of sea, and the hydrus herded him through the opening and out into the sunken city.

Broken walls rose out of the water, thick with barnacles and moss. Tangled sea plants grew in shadowed ponds under low roofs and up stairways. Schools of small fish flashed through window openings. Eels hunted in dark watery chambers. The hydrus herded him toward a stair. He climbed, and found himself in a small room and heard a stone slab pulled across. Again he was a prisoner, and alone.

The room must have been situated high up in the palace, perhaps an attic or storeroom. There was a great stone basin that might have been for bathing, and when he tasted the water it held, it was fresh. He drank gulping, dipping his whole face in.

Around the base of the steps that led down into the sea, oysters and mussels clung in abundance, and it was this as much as the fresh water that made him know the hydrus was prepared to keep him here for some time. He pulled his knife from his belt and ate, stuffing himself, wanting the strength the food would give. It would take all the power he had to subdue the dragon and train her, all his strength, perhaps, simply to make her come to him, for it seemed he had been trying a long time.

Seastrider knew Teb called to her. Dawncloud also knew, and while the young dragon was in a frenzy to go to him and to battle the hydrus, Dawncloud bade her wait; Dawncloud bellowed a challenge to the hydrus and to the dark, her green eyes blazing, and she bade the dragonling wait. She saw her own songs warped and twisted and darkening Teb's mind, so fury held her. She bid Seastrider wait, her voice like a clap of thunder. *He must defeat the hydrus alone!*

The dragonlings looked at her and were still, curling down in the nest, Seastrider shivering.

So they waited, knowing the awesome twisting of the dark songs, knowing Tebriel's acceptance of the dark and, sometimes, his feeble battle. They knew the power that held Tebriel was like a killing fever. They waited, patient as only dragons can be patient, as night followed day and moon followed moon and winter brought raging winds and heaving seas. They felt Teb's chill of body and spirit, his fear. They saw spring begin, a watery sun. They saw the otters searching, in Mernmeth and Pinssra and even as far as Naiheth. But the drowned city where Tebriel was held lay far, far from those submerged villages. They saw the otters give up hope at last, all but the white otter leader. They saw a time when Tebriel seemed lost, sunk steadily into the realm of the dark, grown thin and scowling and without joy. They waited with a dragon's patience, all but Seastrider, who fidgeted and lurched out on the winds and could not be still and sent all her young power to join with Tebriel in his battle. And still they waited. Then at last, they saw Tebriel rise in his spirit and recapture a living strengh. They saw him begin to battle with a new fierceness; they saw his consciousness accept and know, at last, the powerful treachery that gripped his senses.

It was spring. A heavy dark rain sloughed across the sea, beating at the leaden water. Teb lay along the high stone sill that ran along one side of the small stone room, looking out through the thin strip of window that must once have been an arrow slot. He watched the leaden sea and sky and shivered with chill, then felt hot even as the cold wind sloughed in. He had been ill for some days. Behind him in the stone room, rain poured down through a hole in the high roof, into the stone basin, its cold splashing dampening the walls; if he went down to drink, he would be drenched and even colder.

He had been trying all morning to make the dragon come to him. He was furious with the stubbornness of the creature and would rather put it out of his mind. But the hydrus made him keep on, directing his thoughts, demanding, and his own irritable temper mirrored the vicious temper of the hydrus.

He had grown very thin. His body ached often, and he was always cold. He went to sleep at night drowned by exhaustion, desperate and furious at his failure. He did not try to lure or cajole the dragon anymore, or beg her. He demanded. And when he demanded, she seemed to draw farther away. But the hydrus, in turn, demanded, and it would not let him rest.

Teb understood quite well his own importance and the importance of the dragon he must master. They alone could shape the beliefs of the people. The dark could conquer, the dark could enslave, but it was bard and dragon who could make all Tirror love the dark. It was bard and dragon alone who could forge a newly designed history of Tirror and shape people's minds to believe it. It was bard and dragon alone who could weave into the minds of all Tirror a memory of the dark leaders as gods.

"And you will be a god, then, Tebriel," the hydrus had told him, "you will be revered and loved. . . ."

Teb huddled into himself on the cold stone shelf, shivering, then hot. He knew in some distant part of his mind that he was sick, but thought, because the hydrus wanted him to think it, that his aching and discomfort were owing to his failure with the dragon. Its words "You will be a god" were hollow, and its words "You will be revered and loved" puzzled and upset him, so he kept dragging them back into his consciousness and worrying at them. "Revered and loved . . . and loved. . . ."

As the wind grew higher and the rain harder and his fever rose, he left the shelf and huddled down on the bed of rags where he slept. He knew very little now, except the word "loved" pounded with the pulsing of his aching head. Scenes began to come to Teb, born not of song but of the fever. Faces and voices filled his mind, and the word "loved" seemed tangled around them all like the golden threads within a sphere winding and twisting back, with no end. A girl with golden hair, the faces of dark otters, a man with a red beard and hair like the mane of a lion, his mother's face . . . yes . . . loved . . . the King of Auric mounted on a black horse. . . . Father, I love you. . . . Dark furred faces with great brown eyes and then the white face of an otter who looked so deeply at him . . . love . . . Teb twisted and huddled down under the rags, and went weakly to the great basin to drink. The scenes continued and wove themselves into a huge golden sphere of endless pathways that filled his mind so that, as he came out of the fever at last, it was this sphere that held his thoughts and it was these scenes now that wove a skein of memory within him, the dark of the hydrus driven back.

He rose one morning filled equally with the two needs, with the light and the dark. He could sense the hydrus down in the sea and feel its awful power over him. And he understood, for the first time in many months, that its evil must be defeated, and that it was within himself to defeat it. But still there clung within him, too, his awful need for the hydrus and the dark. Then the hydrus spoke to him.

You will not escape, Tebriel. This abberation will not last. You will bring the dragon to me—the young dragon.

I am not your slave. You are defeated now by the very fact of my awareness. But Teb felt afraid, and very weak, and was terrified that the hydrus could, again, drown his mind and twist it. *You are driven out, hydrus! You will not conquer me now!*

The power it sent at him threw him staggering to his knees. He struggled feebly. It held him with terrible strength so he could not rise; sweating and shaking, he fought it now with the last of his physical strength. He could feel its pleasure at his weakness.

But he could feel the young dragon, too, feel her power joining with his own. He stared down with fury at the black pool of sea where the hydrus lay submerged. *You will not have us, dark hydrus. The dragon is of the light and only the light, as am I.*

You will call her, Tebriel. You will make her come to you.

I will not. I will drive you out away from me into the open sea. Fear held him, but the beginning of triumph touched him, too.

If you could drive me out, weak mortal, you would die here. You would die here, alone.

So be it. But you will not have the dragon. Teb stared down at the hydrus's shadow moving beneath the heaving sea. It was then the hydrus laughed, sending a shuddering echo through Teb's mind, so his whole body trembled.

I have the dragon already, Tebriel. It is coming even now.

You lie. You are filled with lies, you know nothing but lies. But Teb, too, could sense a change, could sense the dragons' sudden decision. . . .

"Now," cried Dawncloud to her eager young, "now," and the five dragonlings leaped from the lip of the nest onto Tirror's winds, Seastrider raging in her hatred, vigorous and willful and beating the wind into storm as she fled toward that far sunken city. . . .

Teb sensed them winging between clouds and tried to drive them back, drive Seastrider away. *Go back, go back, do not come here.* . . .

On she came. And in the dark sea below, the hydrus laughed again, and then it came pushing up out of the sea. *The dragon is coming to me, Tebriel. It will belong to me now.*

If it comes at all, it will come to me, and together we will kill you. But, Teb thought, terrified, could the hydrus turn the dragon's powers to darkness, as it had turned his own? He grabbed up his knife where it lay rusting, and stood up, dizzy and unsteady from the sickness, as the hydrus rose out of the dark water, sloughing water up the stone walls.

She does not come to you, Tebriel, but to me.

She comes to me, and you will have to kill me before you have her. Without me she is useless to you. Without me, you cannot control her. And I will never help you.

It reached at him, raging. *If you are of no use to me, then you will die. You will not be used by the light.*

"By the Graven Light," Teb said, staring down at it. "The Graven Light will defeat you—has defeated you. . . ." He chose a spot between the eyes of the center head, his knife ready. The hydrus grabbed for him. Teb leaped with the last of his strength, straddled its huge nose, and thrust the knife directly in between the great eyes. The other two heads reached for him as bone and cartilage shattered. The hydrus screamed; blood spurted over Teb; the creature thrashed, throwing him off. As Teb sprawled on the stone floor, it reached again but went limp, flailing, then dropped down into the shelter of the sea. The sea went red in widening pools. Teb stood shaken, supporting himself against the wall, watching the red thrashing sea as the hydrus slowly pulled the boulder across the sunken portal. It would die now. Or it would mend. If it returned for him, he must be gone. How had he stayed so long in this place, without having the will to escape? When he was sure it had gone, he gathered the last of his strength and he dove, pulling himself down and down along the drowned stairs into the deep, bloodied water.

He explored every inch of the room below, coming up twice to fill his lungs, then diving again. He found at last a tiny hole through which he was just able to push himself, having no idea where it led, or whether the hydrus was there.

He surfaced on the other side of the wall, gasping, and found himself in a huge hall. The sea filled its lower floors. He climbed out, onto a great stone hearth, and took shelter within the huge fireplace. High above, niches gave onto the sky, and he could see the sun's brightness. Sunlight in shafts across the salty pool picked out a stoppered clay jug that might have been floating there the many lifetimes since the land was flooded. When Teb heard the hydrus thrashing and bellowing—not dead at all, but furious at the discovery of his absence—he climbed up inside the chimney.

But the dragons were coming near. He would not be caught and held captive here. He wanted the sky; he wanted to reach out to them.

With a foot on either wall of the chimney, he forced himself up it until his head touched the thick stone slab that sat on its top as a rain guard. This was supported by four short stone pillars, to let the smoke out. Through the holes he could see the bright sky and feel the wind caress him. He began to dig with his knife at the mortar that held the slab. He could hear the hydrus splashing and snuffling in the hall below. It could not reach him here, but could the power of its mind make him fall? He quit digging and remained silent. His leg muscles began to twitch. The bellowing of the hydrus echoed up the chimney, and its mind forced at his, raging. Only now his own strength held steady.

Then he heard another sound that, in spite of the hydrus, set him to digging again.

A high, piercing keening filled the sky, a cry of challenge that drove the last shadows of darkness from his mind and flooded him with joy. He forced the stone off with one frantic thrust and heard it splash into the sea as he lifted himself out and saw the dragons winging between clouds, the immense pearl-hued mother and the five gleaming young. They banked down over him, their green eyes watching him, their iridescent bodies reflecting sun and sea. They circled him, their wings blocking out the sky, and Seastrider so close her wings caressed him. Then Dawncloud wheeled and soared away to drop down over the drowned rooftops, where the shadow of the hydrus lay beneath the sea, its blood still staining the water. Her tongue licked out and she dove, and the five dragonlings followed her.

The sea heaved as the dragons and hydrus battled, thrashing through the depths between broken walls.

Teb clung to the chimney, stricken, clutching his knife as blood boiled up and spread; he watched the bloody trail paint itself out away from the city.

Far out in the sea the disturbance made a geyser. Dawncloud leaped up through foam; then a dragonling rose beside her. Another, another, until four dragonlings were swimming back toward the drowned city. Behind them floated the body of the hydrus, half submerged. The fifth dragonling did not appear. Beside Teb's chimney, Dawncloud crashed up out of the water screaming her pain and her loss for the one dragonling, the one left behind in the jaws of the hydrus, where they floated, dying together. Teb felt Dawncloud's grief as his own, felt Seastrider's weeping as the pale dragonling came to the chimney and wrapped herself around it and laid her head up along his body.

With the sun high overhead they clung so to the ruined chimney, the young dragon and her bard. And then at last Seastrider stirred, put away her grief, and began to study Teb.

19

Teb stared into Seastrider's eyes and felt complete. He marveled at how intricately her scales were woven along her neck and back and along the slim reptilian legs she wrapped around the chimney, scales that could have been crafted of diamonds and of pearls. Her face was slim, her nostrils flared, her two horns white as sunstruck snow, and her cheek felt warm and cool all at once. His mind filled with her songs, and now, together, they made the team for which both had been born. They looked at each other for a long time. Above the sea in the deep afternoon light, Dawncloud circled, keening her agony of mourning, as only a dragon can, for her lost child. The sea rang with her misery, the sunken city absorbed her cry and held it as it held the memory of ages. Moonsong was dead, sleek and beautiful and dear, and not even grown to the full fierce power she should have known, would never know.

It was much later that Dawncloud dropped down out of the sky to dive again among the ruined walls, searching. Teb could see her forcing between stone buildings and down narrow, drowned alleyways, her wings folded close to her body, her white undulating shape curling among watery broken stone and through water shadow, touched by light from the dropping sun. What drew her, now that the hydrus was dead?

"She seeks something," said Seastrider, watching her with a puzzled cock of her head. "Perhaps some old memory, a secret from the ancient city. Perhaps something else." She kneaded her claws into the chimney like a great cat.

They watched Dawncloud slip along the top of a broken wall, to lie looking down into a high attic room, then saw her swerve down into it and disappear. "Come on my back," said Seastrider.

"Can you carry me? You are only young yet."

"Come on my back."

Teb climbed astride as he would mount a pony, and she lifted so fast into the sky she nearly took his breath. He sat clinging between her wings, caught in wonder as the sea fled below, the outlines of the drowned city clear now—the upper and middle baileys and the barbican, the lower and greater halls, the keeping gate and the guard tower all laid out, and the streets surrounding it, the rooftops and the lines of the three old

240

roads leading away. Then suddenly Seastrider dove. Down and down. She came to rest on the edge of a broken wall to look down into the ancient chamber where Dawncloud lay curled upon the stone floor, her head resting on the oak bed. The chamber, quite dry, was furnished. Teb stared down at it with shock: bed and two chairs and even a rug on the floor, its corner protruding underneath Dawncloud's claws. How could a room remain furnished, as if someone had just left it, after hundreds of years of rain and wind and the dampness of the sea? Why hadn't it decayed, like the rest of the city?

There were even blankets on the bed, a cookpot on the hearth, and the charred remains of a fire.

Teb walked along the top of the thick wall, looking down. Dawncloud lay quite still, as if caught in some inner dream, her shoulder against a small cupboard that stood beside the hearth, its door ajar, a touch of red showing inside. It was as he rounded the corner that he saw, down in the water outside the building, the nose of a boat. He moved along the wall until he could look down on its deck, the deck of a small sailing boat.

Her sails had been carefully reefed, but were dark with mold. Her sides were covered with barnacles, but still he could see the bright paint in streaks on her deck and knew she had not sat here for hundreds of years. A few years, maybe. He glanced across at Seastrider perched on the wall watching him, and knew she touched his thoughts. Then he climbed down into the chamber, beside Dawncloud.

He touched the blanket beneath her huge head and ran his hand along her muzzle. He looked around the room, and knew someone had lived here, come here in the little boat to this drowned place. But why? Then he approached the cupboard, caught by the flash of red.

He pulled the door open.

Two gowns hung there. One was red, flame red, with braid around the throat in three rows, and buttons in the shape of scallop shells. He could see his mother in it quite clearly. It had been his favorite dress.

She had been in this room. She had lived in this room.

But when?

She had never been away from them until she left them that last time. She had worn the dress just before she went away.

Was it here she came, then? But why?

And returned to the Bay of Dubla only to drown there? His mind seemed frozen, unable to think clearly.

If she came here in the boat, how did she go away without it?

He stood looking at the dress and at the little room with its blanketed bed and two chairs and the cupboard. In a shelf below the mantel was a blue crock, a small paring knife, and a green plate, all of them familiar, all of them from the palace. The knife handle made of wrapped cord soaked with resin, as old Pakkna always fashioned his knives.

Dawncloud was watching him now, and he knew that she, too, saw his thoughts. All five dragons were watching him, the four young draped along the tops of the walls. He looked at his mother's dress and could see her wearing it before the red flowers of the flame tree.

"Where did she go?" he whispered. "What happened to my mother? She didn't drown in the Bay of Dubla. Where is she?"

Then he sensed Dawncloud's own eagerness and confusion. He sensed her desire, and then visions began to touch him, and he knew, all in a moment, how Dawncloud had lost her bard to murder, how she had slept away her misery in Tendreth Slew, then awakened to seek out a mate.

"But now another bard speaks to me, Tebriel. Somewhere she lives, she who lost her dragon even before my own agony. Somewhere Meriden lives."

"She . . . is a bard?" Teb said hoarsely, hardly believing it. But knowing it was so, and wondering he hadn't guessed before. Her songs, her strength, the way she seemed drawn away sometimes, searching. "She is alive," he cried, caught in wonder. "But where? Where?"

"She is alive, she who turned from the skies in her own misery, and then was drawn back again." Dawncloud reared tall above the broken walls and stared up at the sky and out to sea. Then she writhed her great body down again, into the chamber.

"There is a door in this city, Tebriel. I don't know where, but I will find it. A door that enters, by spells, into the far Castle of Doors. And from that castle, one can enter anywhere, into any world. She is someplace there. Meriden has gone through one of those doors. And I will follow her."

"My mother is alive," he said. "Why did she go? Why would she leave us?"

"She went," Dawncloud said, her voice ringing, "to a mission for all of Tirror. She went hoping to return. Do you not see her boat is still here? She would have sunk it otherwise. She went to give of herself in the saving of Tirror. She went to seek the dragon she thought did not exist anymore on Tirror. And to seek the source of the dark, too, and to learn, if she could learn, how to defeat the dark."

"But how can you know that? You didn't know before, or you would have gone before, to find her."

"Somewhere in this room is a paper with words written on it. The paper tells this message." Dawncloud sighed. "If I were not destined to join with Meriden, if I were not destined to know and love her, I could not know these words." She fixed him with a long green look. "The paper is here, Tebriel. Search for it. And I," she said, stretching up, then winging suddenly to the top of the wall, so the room was filled with the cyclone of her wings, "I must search now, for the door through which she vanished."

She rose up towering, then was over the wall and gone; he heard the tremendous splash of her dive. Then three dragonlings leaped from the wall to follow. Seastrider remained, looking down at him. He stood a moment, his heart pounding; then he stormed up the wall and leaped into the sea and was beating the water, swimming after Dawncloud, choked in the waves she made. He felt Seastrider beside him. "No, Tebriel. No."

"I must," he said, choking, "My mother is there somewhere. . . ."

Dawncloud was so far ahead of him she was almost lost from his sight; the rocking of her passage sent water slapping into his face and up the stone walls. He felt Seastrider's annoyance at him, and her love.

"Come onto my back, then, or we will lose her."

He slipped onto Seastrider's back and she leaped ahead with a twisting speed, her wings beating like great sails. He could not see Dawncloud. And then:

"I'm diving, Tebriel; hold on." Seastrider dropped beneath the sea as he clung, and the water closed over him. Down, down . . . then up again, through a tall arch.

They were in a courtyard. Dawncloud filled the salty pool, rearing up before a dark stone gate all carved with symbols and held with a metal lock. He heard the words she whispered in her silent dragon's voice, then she sang out loudly, so bright and wild he trembled. The dragonlings were singing with her, a strange song, not a ballad; this was a dragon's command, and magical. The stone doors opened, and he could see nothing beyond but white mist, moving mist. Then Dawncloud was through. He leaped from Seastrider's back to follow, but Dawncloud turned in the doorway, the huge silvery bulk of her filling it, and faced down at him, her great mouth open in a dragon's terrible scream, so close to him he saw flame starting way back in her throat. "Stay back, Tebriel. Do not come here."

"I must come. She is my mother."

"All of Tirror is your mother. All of Tirror needs you and Seastrider. You would only hinder me here. How can I travel as I must, search as I must, with a small human companion? She is my bard, Tebriel. If she can be found, I will find her. A million worlds lie beyond this mist. I would lose you.

"Stay with Seastrider here. See to the tasks you were born to. . . ." And then with one thrashing motion she was gone into the mist, and the great doors swung closed again.

He paddled close to Seastrider, heartbroken. Then he slid onto her back, sadly, silently, and they returned to the small room where his mother had slept, the four dragonlings close together now, steeped in the sadness of losing their own mother.

"We sang the ancient song for opening," Nightraider said, filled with wonder.

"We sang it all together in our minds," said Wind-caller.

"It opened for her," said Nightraider. "And she went through."

"She will be through the Castle of Doors by now," said Seastrider. "She will be out into another world by now," she said sadly. "Searching for Meriden."

In the little room, as the dragonlings lay along the top of the wall, Teb began to search for the small bit of paper or parchment that would hold his mother's handwriting.

He found it at last, tucked down between an empty wooden cask and an iron pot, beneath the oak bed. He knew it at once, and wondered why he hadn't guessed before. It was not a slip of parchment but his mother's brass-bound journal that she had kept just as Camery kept a diary. His mother's journal, locked, and the key missing.

He supposed he could break the lock, but he was loath to. Dawncloud had told him the message, surely all of it. He put the little book in the pocket of his breechcloth, then climbed the wall and down again, to examine the boat, as Seastrider watched from above.

The boat's name could still be seen, *Merlther's Bird*, then the name of her port, Bleven. Merlther Blish's boat, reported lost months before his mother went away.

"She deceived us," he said, fingering the cracked

letters. "She meant to go away all the time. She lied to us."

Seastrider sailed down to land beside him, dwarfing the boat and weighting it to its gunwales. She rubbed her cheek against his. "She did what she must. For Tirror. You do not listen well to my mother." She was annoyed with him. He regarded her evenly.

"My mother said she went to battle the dark. Do you not listen? She deceived you only because it was required of her, because it would be wisest. Not because she didn't love you. There was no deceit in her heart, Tebriel."

He stood quietly, looking at the little boat that had been pulled in so carefully between the stone walls in this shadowed watery world. And he knew Seastrider was right. She nuzzled his hand until he put his arm around her. At last he let wonder touch him and the true joy that his mother was alive.

It was later, when he had returned to the little room that had been her last chamber in this world, that he began to wonder if his father had known all along. That she was not dead. That she had meant to go away in this fashion.

He must have hated the dark all the more, because it made it necessary for Meriden to go away. He must have felt terrible anger that he could not help her. That he must stay and guard Auric, while she did battle in a world so far away he might never see her again. Had he known, guessed, that they would never be together again?

Seastrider soared off the top of the wall and dropped down into the room beside him.

"How can Dawncloud ever find her?" he said sadly.

"It will not be an easy search. Perhaps there are vibrations out among those worlds, just as there are in the sea." She curled down around Teb and lowered her head on her back, making a cocoon for him. "Rest, Tebriel. When night grows darkest, we will go home. To the Lair. Tonight, Tebriel, you will sleep among dragons, at the top of the highest peaks."

"And tomorrow?" he said, his excitement rising.

"Tomorrow . . . and tomorrow . . . we will begin to assess the dark, Tebriel. We will begin to discover how best we can battle it, to bring Tirror back to truth. We will begin to strengthen our powers—of creating image and memory and hope through song. We will begin to discover other powers."

"What other powers? The opening of doors . . . ?"

"Perhaps. And perhaps we can master the magic of shape shifting, and perhaps other ways to confuse the dark."

He leaned back against her warm, jeweled side and felt the strength of bard and dragon, teamed, and thought that, with training together, they might know more power than he had imagined. Together they would make song, would shape Tirror's true past for those who lived today, and he knew that this was their one great weapon. For to know what has been is to know what can be. This was what the dark must destroy if it would win the minds of its slaves. If it would create a willing acceptance of slavery. As the night drew down, and the thin moon rose, Seastrider said, "We will go now," and they swept out across the sea toward Windthorst and Fendreth-Teching, four bright dragons, one carrying her bard, he caught in the wonder of this first flight, caught in the wonder of beginning.

They passed over Nightpool in darkness, high against the stars where no earthbound creature could see them. Yet in the empty meeting cave, before the sacred clam shell, Thakkur saw. This vision was clear and strong. The white otter smiled, and put from him his loneliness for Tebriel, in the knowledge that Teb was now, in this time in the world, exactly where he belonged.

Above, so close to stars, Teb grinned too as he stared up at the heavens, then down toward the dark earth below him, and he thought, *Tonight I will sleep among dragons.* The night wind washed around him, stirred by Seastrider's powerful wings, and he felt her laughing pleasure, like his own.

We are together now, Tebriel, and soon my brothers and sister may find their bards, and my mother return with Meriden, and we will be an army, then, to challenge the lords of the dark.